Dreams of an Endless Summer

Josh Magnotta

For Victoria.

Chapter 1

"Eli, wake up."

Cali nudged him with her foot. Eli groaned and stirred slightly. Cali tugged on the blanket and pulled it off his shoulder.

"Come on Eli, we can't stay in bed all day," she said as she pushed him gently.

"We could," he said, his voice heavy with sleep. He stretched long and deep, extending his arms in front of him, his feet pressed against the tightly tucked sheet.

Cali pushed him a little harder, rolling him onto his stomach and close to the edge.

"Don't make me do it Eli," she said.

"Do it, you won't," he replied.

"Come on, Eli."

"This is why I don't like sleeping."

"Why?"

"Cause you have to wake up," he said.

"Well, you can't sleep forever," Cali said.

"No. But it's just nice dreaming. Anything is possible."

"Oh? What were you dreaming?" Cali asked.

Eli slowly closed his eyes again.

"You're just going to ignore me?" Cali asked.

"I'm not ignoring you, I'm sleeping."

"No, come on. We need to get out of bed," Cali said. "Don't make me push you."

Eli's eyes were still closed, a smile pulled at the corner of his lips.

"I see how it is," Cali said. "Alright. I tried to be nice."

She threw the blanket back and pushed Eli hard. He rolled off the bed. As he fell, he grabbed Cali's arm and pulled her down with him. They tumbled to the carpet and Cali pinned Eli to the floor.

"Good one," she said. She planted her hands on either side of his head and gazed down at him. Her hair fell in curtains as she leaned close. The sweet almond scent of her shampoo enveloped Eli. He ran his fingers through her hair. Cali smiled and lowered her head, her hair brushed against his cheeks. He closed his eyes and wrapped his hands around her, pulling her closer. She kissed him once on the forehead.

Eli smiled and opened his eyes. Cali's bright green eyes scanned his face as her fingers swept over his cheek and across his parted lips. Eli watched as she admired him, then he closed his eyes again and let the feeling of her touch consume him.

Her fingers were soft on his skin, touching, investigating. She traced a line along his jaw and down his neck, passing over his Adam's apple down to the hollow point just above his collarbone. Then, Eli felt the warmth of her lips on his neck; her gentle breath against his skin sent his heart racing.

Deliberately slow, each kiss sent a chill down Eli's spine. As she migrated closer to his lips, she paused briefly. There was pressure between them. Eli felt it, hot and tense, like the heat of a summer day just before a thunderstorm. Cali's lips trembled and Eli's heart pounded in his chest. Nervous excitement punctuated the moment. They hesitated. Then, like that first roll of thunder that ushers in the rain, their lips touched.

The pressure melted away and there was nothing between them.

Sometime later, they walked down the shallow hillside to the river. Water gurgled as it lapped over rocks. In the middle of the stream the water deepened and the stones along the bottom disappeared below the green-blue water.

Cali rolled the bottoms of her jeans halfway up her calves and kicked off her shoes. Eli did the same. Together they waded out into the river. Cali's hand tensed in Eli's as the water rushed over their feet and splashed their legs.

"A little further out?" she asked.

She turned to Eli, her eyes flashing brilliantly in the light reflecting off the water.

"Up to you. I feel good right here," Eli said.

"Okay. I'm good here too," she said.

Eli took a step closer and slid his arm around Cali's waist. She nestled closer, her hip pressed against his thigh.

"I love it down here," she said. It's so calm."

"If you had to pick, would you rather live down here on the river or up high in the mountains?" Eli asked.

On the other side of the river a cardinal cheered and somewhere further along a robin called. Crickets chirped in the tall grass. The sounds of summer played on endlessly.

"It'd be hard to build a house right on the river," Cali said.

"Okay, not on the river, but next to it. Like you can step out your back door and walk to it," Eli said.

"I don't know," Cali said. She turned slightly to look into his eyes.

After a moment of thought she answered.

"The river is nice," she started. "I love the sound of the water and the animals. Could you imagine falling asleep to that every night?"

Eli nodded listening as the water rolled and splashed along its course and the birds continued their songs.

"But the mountains are great too," Cali said. "Like, the hills around here seem small, but when you get to the top of one and then look back it kinda takes your breath away. It's like you almost don't realize you are going higher and higher until you reach the top. I can't even imagine what it's like out West near the Rockies. That must be crazy."

She sighed and shrugged her shoulders.

"I don't know, I can't pick. You?" she asked.

"I would pick the mountains. But, I would make sure there was a river right next to my house, then I can have the best of both," Eli said.

Cali flicked his ear.

"That's cheating," she said. "But I like the sound of it. Now, do you have a cabin or just a regular house?" she asked.

"Cabin. Simple, but efficient. I don't need much room inside. Anyway, why would I want to stay inside when I've got a river in my backyard and I live on top of a mountain?"

"Yeah, that's true. I think I'd say the same. As long as it's comfortable enough and warm in the winter, who cares how big it is?" Cali said.

"Right?" Eli agreed.

They stood in silence for a few minutes watching the water meander by. Cali leaned against Eli and for the moment they were lost to the world, just the two of them alone in the river.

"I can't wait," Cali said.

Startled from a trance, Eli turned to her.

"For what?" he asked.

"When we can have that. When it isn't just a dream," Cali said.

"Someday," Eli said. His voice rang hollow. Cali sighed.

"It seems like a long time now, but maybe someday we'll look back and realize, it wasn't that long at all."

Then she took Eli's hand and leaned down to pick up a stone from the riverbed. Eli kept her steady as she grabbed the stone and then stood back up.

"Perfect for skipping, no?" Cali asked, turning a small round rock over in her hand before handing it to Eli.

"Yeah," he said as he inspected it. "This is a good one. Let's see what you got."

Cali took the stone back and looked out across the river. Then, she bent slightly at the hip and stretched her arm to her side. In a quick snap of the wrist she flung the stone flat across the water and watched as it skipped over the waves before finally sinking near the opposite bank.

"I counted ten," she said.

"Yea, that was a great throw," Eli said.

"You can't beat it," Cali said.

"I can, but I won't," Eli said with a smile.

Cali grinned, "You can't and you know it."

"Alright, if you insist."

Eli grabbed a stone and gazed across the river looking for a calm section of water. He eyed a spot about halfway across. He lowered his shoulder and flung the rock, keeping his arm parallel to the river.

He watched as the stone skimmed across the calm water leaving ripples in its wake. It was a perfect throw. The rock skipped across to the other side and came to rest in the muddy bank.

"Fourteen?" Eli asked.

"I think so," Cali said. "I can beat that."

Time slipped away as the two became lost in that perfect summer bliss.

It was evening before they finally emerged from the river. Their pants were soaked above the knee, but neither seemed to mind. It had been a perfect afternoon.

They walked along the bank that followed the river on the northern side of town. Hand in hand they wandered through knee-high grass until they reached the bridge on the outskirts of their small community. There, they made their way down to Main Street and headed toward Cali's house. The streetlights were just starting to flicker to life and the sun was dipping over the hills to the west. The sky was purple above and, on the horizon, brilliant orange and red.

Cali's Mom's sedan was parked in the driveway. Her Dad's truck wasn't home yet.

"He must've had to stay late today," Cali said as they took the steps to the front door.

"Wonder when he will get home?" Eli mused.

"Probably not until late," Cali said. "He'll be tired. He'll probably go right to bed."

A smile played at the corner of Eli's lips.

"What are you saying?" Eli asked.

Cali met his eyes.

"Nothing. I'm just stating facts," she said.

"Those aren't exactly facts," Eli said.

"They are."

"Okay," Eli said. "Let's say they are. What do they mean?"

Cali smiled and lifted her eyebrows ever so slightly.

"Wait a couple hours," she said quietly. "But not before ten."

Eli smiled. He leaned close and kissed Cali on the cheek.

"Ten o'clock," he said with a nod.

"The back porch, I'll leave the door unlocked," Cali whispered before stealing a quick kiss on the lips.

"I'll see you then."

Chapter 2

Eli trotted home, down Main Street toward the West end of town. Here, the streetlights were spaced out and the houses all seemed to blend into the same ugly shade of gray. He turned left and slowed to a walk. He ignored the awkward stares from the neighbors and kept his head down, his eyes focused on the pavement.

As he neared the end of the street, the ammonia stench of cat urine crept into his nose. A cat scurried past and bounded up the steps of a nearby porch where it joined three others. Eli could just make out the shine of their eyes in the dwindling light. Old Lady Willow, the cat lady of all cat ladies. Eli rarely saw her. Apparently, her reclusive nature appealed to her feline friends, there seemed to be more cats creeping around her house every day.

How many cat's does she have? Too many, Eli thought.

He kept walking, but the cat odor didn't leave his nose until he climbed the steps to his grandmother's house. Then, it was replaced with a new odor, stale beer and whiskey. Eric was home.

Eli sighed and walked inside.

His grandmother was huddled in her recliner, a blanket over her legs, her glasses perched on the end of her nose and a diet soda in a glass on the end table beside her.

She turned her gaze from the TV as Eli came inside. She blinked a couple times before she realized who it was.

"Eli, I was startin' to worry 'bout ya," she said. "There's mac' n' cheese on the stove if you're hungry."

"I'm good, thanks grandma," Eli said as he walked across the room to give his grandmother a hug. She kissed him on the cheek. Eli took a seat on the couch next to her recliner.

From the corner of the room, hidden in the shadows, there was the shuffle of papers and the crunch of an aluminum can.

Eli peered into the dark.

The curtains were drawn and the light from the TV shined sporadically in that corner of the room, leaving Eric mostly hidden in the dark. A waist-high bookshelf separated that section of the living room from the rest. It was a reading corner. A cozy little nook where one could curl up with a nice book and pass the evening. Only, Eric wasn't doing much reading.

"Tanks gwandma. Tanks gwandma. Tank you, tank you, tank you gwandma," Eric's high-pitched mocking voice came from the corner. He laughed. His laughter cut short by an obnoxiously loud belch.

Eli's grandmother turned toward him and shook her head.

"Just be nice," she whispered.

Eli glanced down and saw that his fists were clenched tight. He relaxed his hands and laid them in his lap. He took a deep breath, then he leaned back and attempted to ignore his older brother.

Eli tried to focus on the television. But every few minutes his eyes would wander toward the corner where his brother sat hidden in the shadows. Why was he even here? Eli wondered.

The television flashed blue and red. For a brief moment Eli saw his brother's face, haggard and thin, his blue eyes striking even in his inebriated state. The lights dimmed and Eric disappeared in the dark once more.

"How long has he been here?" Eli whispered.

His grandmother turned to him and shrugged her shoulders. "A few hours."

"He's not staying here?" Eli asked.

"Just for a little while, Eli," she said. "Just till he can get back on his feet."

"No. No, why do you let him do this?" Eli asked.

"He's your brother, Eli. Have a little respect."

"Respect? He doesn't respect himself, why should I respect him?" Eli said, his voice growing louder.

"Eli, enough. This is my house and your brother is welcome here, whether you like it or not," his grandmother said. "Besides, haven't I raised you better than that? Your brother needs love, not hate."

"He'd be easier to love if he wasn't always drunk," Eli spat.

He didn't care if Eric heard him or not. In fact, he kind of hoped he did.

"Eli!" his grandmother yelled.

"What? He always does this," Eli started, rising to his feet. "He is going to stay here and leech off you long enough for you to think he might actually be better. Then he'll find someone dumb enough to sleep with him and he'll be gone again and you'll be hurt. It always happens that way."

"Eli enough!"

"Grandma, you know how this goes," Eli said.

"Lower your voice," his grandmother said.

"I don't care if he hears me."

"Fine, that's your problem. But don't you ever raise your voice with me, Eli," she said. Her voice cut quick to the heart. Eli realized he'd lost himself in his anger.

"I'm sorry," he grumbled and sat back down.

"Eli, it's not for us to decide his actions. We just need to love him," she said.

"How can I love someone who is never here? Even when he's here, he's too far gone to talk to," Eli said.

"He's still your brother."

"He isn't a brother to me."

Eli's grandmother moved fast and struck him hard across the face with her open palm.

"Don't you ever say that again," she said through gritted teeth.

Her words stung more than her slap, nonetheless Eli raised his hand to his cheek. His skin was warm beneath his hand.

"Your brother is still alive, Eli," she said. "What I'd give to talk to my brother again. Your brother has flaws. I know that. Still, we need to love him all the same. He will come around. And when he does you'll be glad you didn't turn your back on him."

"But how can I love him when he treats you like this?"

"Eli, I'm not as frail as you make me out to be. I'll be just fine," she said with a smile. "But I wouldn't mind a hand getting upstairs."

Eli smiled and helped the old woman to her feet and across the living room away from the corner where

Eric sat. Eli helped his grandmother up the stairs and to her room. As he closed the door she bid him goodnight.

"Sweet dreams, Eli," she said. "And please be nice to Eric. If not for your own sake, then for me."

"Alright. Goodnight, grandma," he said.

"Goodnight, Eli. I love you."

"I love you too."

He made his way softly back down the stairs expecting to find Eric in the same chair on the opposite side of the room. But as he stepped into the living room he noticed, Eric was gone.

Eli went out to the kitchen and found his brother seated at the table the whiskey bottle clutched in his right hand.

"Sit down," Eric said.

Eli hesitated, then took a seat across from his brother.

"I missed you," Eric said. He reached out to ruffle Eli's hair, but Eli shrugged him off.

"I thought bout you and grams every day," Eric said.

He eyed Eli, his head wavering slightly. Then he took a swig from the bottle. Eli's stomach turned as he watched.

Eric slammed the bottle down and sighed.

"I don' mean ta hurt ya,'" Eric said.

Eli nodded.

"I heard ya talkin'," Eric mumbled. "I know what ya think a me."

"No, you don't," Eli said.

"Lissen. It don' matter. Eli. It don't matter. I know what ya wanted to say. And that's the same ain't it?"

"And what's that?' Eli said.

"Lissen. Don't be like that, Eli. Alright? Don't be like that."

"Me? What about you? Showing up out of nowhere, drunk again. What do you expect from me? Open arms? You want me to say how much I missed you?"

"Wouldn't that be somethin'," Eric said.

"Screw you. You aren't gonna be here long anyway," Eli said. He pushed his chair from the table and started to get up.

Eric waved his hand over the table and shook his head.

"No, no. Sit down. Sit down," he mumbled.

Eli stood and glanced down at his brother.

"Eli please. I just wanna talk fer a minute," Eric said. "Please, Eli. Please."

Eli looked at his brother. The sweat shining on his brow, his greasy hair pushed back so it didn't fall in his bloodshot eyes. Eric gazed up at Eli, his eyes unfocused and his head bobbing softly. But then he heard his grandmother's voice. *Please, be nice to Eric.*

Eli sighed and sat back down.

"Thank you," Eric said. "Thank you, Eli. I just need someone to talk to ya know?"

"Right. What do you need to say?" Eli asked.

"It's nothin', but it is kinda a big deal. I just can't tell grams. You can't tell her neither, okay?" Eric said.

"We'll see," Eli said.

"No, it don't work like that. You gotta promise me, Eli. Don't tell grams."

"Okay, what is it?"

"Here," Eric stumbled out of his chair and shuffled across the kitchen to the cabinet. He leaned on the counter and then opened the cabinet door and took out a coffee mug. He shambled back to the table and sat back down. He closed his eyes and wavered there in his chair for a moment. He blinked back awake and poured whiskey in the mug. Then he looked up at Eli and slid the mug across the table.

"No, I'm not drinking with you," Eli said.

Eli pushed the mug to the side. He raised his eyes to meet his brother's red glare.

"I want you to," Eric said.

"No, I don't want any," Eli refused.

"It's jus a lil' bit. It won't hurt ya," Eric said.

"No."

"Eli."

"What? I'm not drinking it." Eli said.

"Fine, whatever you want," Eric said. He glanced at the mug and shook his head.

"What were you gonna say?" Eli asked.

"I wish you would just drink it. It'd be easier that way. Why do ya always have to fight?" Eric said.

"You didn't have anything to say did you?"

Eric turned his eyes from the mug and met Eli's stare. His eyes were focused. He laid his hands on the table.

"I have news," he said.

Eli nodded and waited.

"I'm gonna be a dad."

Eli sat up in his chair and leaned forward.

"What?" he said.

"Yea. Baby should be here at the end of December. A Thanksgiving baby. Ain't that something?" Eric said.

"You mean Christmas," Eli said. "Who's the mom?"

"You don't know her," Eric said.

"Are you guys together?"

"Sorta. We were, then her old boyfriend moved back into town," Eric said. "She hasn't told him yet. She's been hiding it well. But he's gonna find out soon."

"What are your plans?" Eli asked.

"I don't know," Eric said. "I can't support a kid."

"You'll have to."

"But you don't understand."

"You'll have to get a job. Maybe two," Eli said.

"No, that's not it . . . I'll get a job," Eric struggled to speak. He shrugged his shoulders. "I can work. That's nothin'. But, yea, it's messed up. It's gonna be a such a mess."

"What?" Eli asked.

"It's not gonna to be right," Eric said, tears forming at the corners of his eyes.

"What do you mean?"

"The baby isn't growin' right," he said. "We don't know if it's going to make it."

Eli watched the tears start to fall down his brother's face. Eric reached for the bottle, but Eli grabbed his hand instead.

"What did the doctor say?" Eli asked.

"He doesn't know," Eric said. "He said it didn't look good. They did the jelly thing where they take photos of the baby. And he said it was growin' slower than it should."

"It's still early, though right? There's time for it to change. I think they all grow different right?" Eli said.

"I don't know," Eric said. He laid his head on his forearm. "I don't know."

"We'll get it figured out," Eli said. "It'll all be alright."

He took his hand off his brother's and stayed there at the table until eventually Eric dozed off. Eli took the whiskey bottle and put it in the cupboard. Not gone, but out of reach for now. He poured the mug in the sink before going out to the front porch and sitting on the steps.

Eric couldn't be a father, Eli thought. He can't even take care of himself. Eli ran his hand through his hair and shook his head. Then he gazed up into the night sky. It was a dark purplish color as it transitioned to night. The stars shined bright overhead, the moon just a sliver of white above the horizon.

All that space, all that separation. Yet those distances were a problem for civilizations well beyond human understanding. Our struggles are still small; money, love, religion. We have a long way to go before we have to worry about traveling between stars, Eli thought. Hell, just getting to another planet is a big step for us.

Eli glanced back at the door behind him. Yea, we have problems enough right here, without worrying about traveling the stars.

What was he going to do?

What am I going to do?

It's not my kid, but he's my brother. Drunkard and a mooch as he is, he is still my brother. I'll have to help, whatever that means, Eli thought.

He's going to have to quit drinking though. I can't be expected to raise his kid while he gets drunk every night. That can't happen. I'll help, but he's going to have to face that problem before he can be a father. I don't understand why he drinks anyway. Maybe we should figure that out first, Eli thought.

Eli turned his attention back to the stars and wondered. So much distance. So much time. As he looked up, his heart ached for the one person with whom he never quarreled. The afternoon with her had passed too quickly. How much longer before he could be with her again?

Eli checked his watch. It was still only 9:20. He had a little bit of time before he could wander down the street to Cali's. It was only a short walk. Still, he wished he didn't have to wait.

Everything was always about waiting. Waiting for the clock to move, waiting to be with Cali, waiting always waiting. And then when the moment arrived, whatever it was, it was always over too fast. It would be that way all summer and before he knew it Eli would be back in school for senior year. One more year. Then, what?

He still didn't know.

He didn't really want to think about it tonight either. There would be time enough to think about it later, at least, that's what he told himself. That time was dwindling, but he still had all summer and even a few months of senior year to come up with a plan. He would figure it out.

Eli gazed down the street. It was a mostly quiet night, but there were still a few people milling about, mostly on their front porches having a smoke or drinking. Eli watched as a person a few houses down took a long drag on a cigarette, their face illuminated in the orange glow. He watched the cigarette flicker and fade before eventually going out. Then the person lit another one and Eli turned his attention elsewhere.

Coming from somewhere further down the street, Eli heard the muffled cries of people arguing. He couldn't make out the words. The person smoking could probably hear everything. Was that why they were on their porch, to listen in on someone fighting?

Wouldn't that be a shame, Eli thought. But then again, was it really any different than distracting oneself with a television show? Eli wondered. There was a level of separation with television, the problems were distant. You could maybe relate to a situation, but there was a remoteness. You were always detached even when you were invested. But when the fighting was taking place next door, well, then there was almost something tangible about it, like you could reach out and touch it. Maybe in the end it was just a better distraction, a way to escape one's own problems.

Eli picked at the frayed fabric of his jeans as he thought.

Distraction. Perhaps, that's all some people had, distractions from their own problems. I guess distractions could manifest themselves in different ways, he thought. You could listen to someone fighting next door, you could drown your troubles in whiskey. It was all just a form of distraction, a way out of your own head.

What a pity, he thought. That life should amount to no more than that for some people. Just looking for something, anything to focus on to forget that you're wasting away the days. There was no hope in that life, just a sad realization that this was it. This was as good as it gets.

Eli plucked a loose thread from his jeans. Then, he stood up and stretched deep.

A glance at his watch told him only ten minutes had passed, it was still too early to walk to Cali's, but he couldn't sit here any longer.

Chapter 3

A slight breeze blew, shuffling the hair hanging over Eli's brow. He sighed, relishing the air against his skin. It was a warm night. It finally felt like summer was settling in for good.

He walked down a side street a couple blocks over from his grandma's. This street was a little quieter. Or maybe the sounds were just different. There wasn't any screaming, or rather, there wasn't any fighting, at least none noticeable from the sidewalk where Eli tread. There were screams, but they were the pleasant joyful sounds of children yipping in excitement as they caught a lightning bug or played a game of tag. They were the screams of happiness and seemingly endless childhood.

Eli smiled.

As he walked along the sidewalk, he noticed what seemed to him a peculiar absence of litter. There were no cigarette butts or soda and beer cans. There were no empty plastic bags floating aimlessly like ghosts without a home. No, the sidewalk here was clean. As were the lawns. Grass, cut short and trimmed close along the border of the sidewalk, was pleasing to look at and seemed almost soft and inviting. Eli glanced over his shoulder. There didn't seem to be anyone nearby. So, he took a hesitant step onto the freshly groomed yard. The ground wasn't hard or resisting, in fact, quite the opposite, it seemed to give way ever so slightly and cushion his foot. Eli took two more steps out onto the lawn, smiling to himself.

The sweet smell of a barbeque tickled his nose. He closed his eyes imagined a family out back, kids playing, adults gathered on a patio talking. Calm, peaceful, secure, everything seemed perfect.

There was a squeal of laughter from somewhere nearby. Eli opened his eyes. He glanced at the house and saw the front door swing open. He quickly stepped back out onto the sidewalk and continued on his way. Nobody was looking for trouble.

He was only a couple streets over from his grandma's house, but to Eli, this may as well have been a different town. He imagined he could live in a place like this one day. Maybe it was a simple life, but that was fine. A house with a nice lawn and kids laughing enjoying life, what was wrong with that? That would be nice, just living the dream.

"Someday," Eli said.

He continued down the road until he came to Main Street. He stopped beneath a streetlamp to look at his watch. It was close enough to 10:00 and getting darker. He would slowly head to Cali's and still be a couple of minutes early.

While he was about a block away, Eli spied the back end of Cali's dad's truck in the driveway. A construction worker, Cali's dad drove a big white truck with tool boxes on the back and a steel grate along the front bumper. Eli never rode in it, but he imagined it was probably fun to drive, sitting up high looking down on the rest of the traffic. That had to be cool.

As Eli came to Cali's house he walked quietly through the side yard and around the back. Cali would meet him on the back porch. And sure enough, as he rounded the side of the house, there she was sitting on the steps waiting for him.

"You're on time," she said with a smile.

"I couldn't be late," he said.

Cali hopped down the steps and leaped into Eli's arms. They tumbled in a warm embrace and fell lightly on the soft grass. Cali rested her head on Eli's arm. For some time, they laid together, listening to the soft rhythm of each other's heart amid the quiet whisperings of the night. Eventually, their lips found each other, the soft beating of their hearts quickened. Around them, the night became still, the gentle twilight orchestra faded to a soft lullaby. As they parted, the scent of Cali's vanilla perfume lingered and Eli breathed deep.

Cali turned to face the night sky. The moon was just a thin sliver and the stars shined bright. The dense band of light that made up the Milky Way streaked across the heavens like the flourishing final touch of an artist's brush on canvas.

"Beautiful isn't it?" she asked.

"Yea, it is," he said.

For a moment there wasn't anything else to say, they just laid there together taking it all in. Eli reached out and found Cali's hand. Her skin was warm and smooth as he ran his fingers over the back of her hand.

And for a little while, Eli forgot about the troubles with his brother. Those were real problems, tactile problems that couldn't just be solved with a hug. Times like this with Cali were different. To Eli, it seemed like they were in their own little world. No, different than that, he thought. It was more like everything felt wispy, ethereal, sort of apart from everything else. And yet, there was the very real feeling of Cali's hand in his. He was here in this moment, but this moment felt distant and somehow close at the same time. He couldn't describe it to Cali, it was something that had to be felt. So, instead of trying to figure out whatever weird scientific reason was behind the feeling, Eli just enjoyed the moment and let everything else fade away.

Cali turned onto her side, and shifted her attention to Eli. Eli followed suit and met her eyes.

"What do you want to talk about tonight?" Cali asked.

"I don't know. You pick," Eli said.

"You're boring," Cali teased.

"I'm not," Eli said. "I'm courteous."

"Oh, ok. Very gentlemanly," Cali said.

"Yes, very gentlemanly indeed."

Cali giggled.

"We don't have to talk about anything I guess, we could just be."

"You said that was boring," Eli said.

"No, I said you were boring," Cali said.

Eli smiled and shook his head, but the smile faded quickly as thoughts of his brother crept back into his mind. Why did Eric have to ruin everything?

"What are you thinking?" Cali asked.

"It's nothing," Eli said.

"No, it's something," Cali said.

She gently touched his cheek, waiting for him to say more.

Eli sighed. It was no use trying to hide it from Cali. She knew him too well.

"Eric came home today," he said simply.

"Oh," Cali sighed. "Was he as bad as last time?"

Eli couldn't compare one time to another. It was always the same and never good. But there was more this time.

"I guess it was kinda worse this time," Eli said. "He told me he is gonna be a dad."

"Are you serious?"

"Yeah. I don't know what to think. He hasn't told grandma yet and he wants me to keep it secret," Eli said.

"How is he going to take care of a baby? He can't even take care of himself," Cali said.

"I know," Eli agreed.

"Are you going to tell your grandma?" Cali asked.

"I don't know," Eli said. "I mean one of us will have to tell her eventually. I don't want to be the one to do it. Honestly, I don't even know why he told me," Eli said.

Eli rolled onto his back again. Cali did the same.

"Maybe he trusts you," Cali offered.

"No," he sighed. "I don't think so. We were never really close like that."

"Maybe not to you," Cali said.

"I don't know."

"Well, there's nothing you can do about it right now," Cali said.

"Yeah," he agreed.

Eli took Cali's hand again. Their fingers wove together and Cali squeezed slightly.

As they admired the night sky above, Eli battled a flurry of conflicting thoughts in his head. He wanted to enjoy this peace with Cali, and at a surface level he did, but inside he was consumed with the negativity surrounding Eric. Much as he wanted to let those thoughts disappear, he couldn't. Overwhelming fear of the future, a future he couldn't control, leeched from his happiness and left him feeling empty and confused. Cali tried to soothe his angst, to little avail. There was nowhere else Eli wanted to be, but when they finally said goodnight he couldn't help but feel his worry had stolen some of their joy.

Chapter 4

Once home from Cali's, Eli wandered up to his bedroom. He didn't stop to look where Eric was, it didn't matter. Eli plopped onto his bed, but struggled to sleep. His head buzzed with thoughts of Cali. He didn't deserve her affection. He only brought her down. He stole what was good in her and made it less. How could he tell her that? She loved him, but he wasn't good for her. She was so much better than this town. And yet I embody this town, Eli thought. Just wishful thinking, hoping for a miracle, a lottery-sized change of fortune that would never come and could never truly fix the problems of this life. That mindset was buried deep. Cali could do so much more without him.

Eventually his eyes fluttered closed and he fell into a fitful sleep.

When he woke, he stumbled out of bed foggy headed and feeling like he hadn't slept at all. He shuffled downstairs. His grandma was already at the kitchen table with a cup of coffee and a crossword puzzle. Eli glanced at the coffee maker, saw she had made a full pot, poured himself a mug, and sat at the table with her.

"How long have you been up?" he asked.

"Well, that's the second pot I've made this morning," she said. Eli glanced at his mug.

"You drank a whole pot already?"

"Yea, I'd say I been up a couple hours," she said.

Eli watched the elderly woman fill in a line on her puzzle. She closed her eyes and tapped her lips as she thought. After a moment she opened her eyes and filled in another space.

"Gram, you shouldn't drink that much coffee," Eli said.

She set her pencil down and took a sip from her mug.

"I'm fine. Hell, I been drinking coffee since I was a kid," she said. "I'm just starting to wake up after one pot."

"Seriously?"

"Lemme tell ya a story," she said, closing her word search.

She stretched her hands, her gnarled old fingers cracked. She sighed and rubbed her knuckles before taking a sip from her mug and spinning her tale.

"When I was a baby, my oldest brother used to have to watch us little ones. I was the second youngest and he musta been twelve or thirteen at the time. It was a different time back then, my Pa was always on the road and Ma was working double shifts at the factory to make ends meet, so us kids had to figure things out on our own."

"How many siblings did you have?" Eli asked.

"Five of us total. There's only two of us left though. My sister lives down south. She got outta town right after school and never looked back. She was smart."

She nodded and a smile touched her cheeks. Then she took another sip of coffee and continued with her story.

"Anyway, Ralph being the oldest, he was in charge. So, every morning he would have to make sure my two other older siblings were around for school and that me and my baby sister were cared for. I was the fussy one. Always was. I was the pickiest eater you ever saw. I feel bad Ralph had to deal with me, he didn't know what to do, he was just a kid himself. Well one morning, I think he was at his wit's end and didn't realize what he was doing, but he ended up putting a whole cup of coffee in front of me for breakfast. Mind you, I'm only about two at the time. Anyway, I ended up drinking that whole cup before Ralph realized what he'd done. I don't know what surprised him more, that I actually ate, well, drank something for breakfast, or that I downed a whole mug of coffee! Either way, he found out that was the only thing I would eat. So, every morning after that's what he gave me," she said with a laugh.

Eli smiled, but shook his head.

"That's not healthy," he said.

"Nothin's healthy. Seems just about everything's gonna kill ya," she said.

Eli shrugged. What was the point of arguing? He took a sip of coffee then leaned back in his chair. His grandmother opened her word search again and set back to work.

"Eric still here?" he asked.

"Out in the living room," she said, not lifting her eyes from her book.

"You think he's going to stay long?" he asked.

"Oh, I don't know," she answered. "Probably. I'm sure he's in some kind of trouble."

She took a drink from her mug then looked across the table at Eli. Her old eyes searched him. After a moment she smiled and went back to her puzzle.

"Don't you even tell me," she said. "I don't want to know."

"I don't know what you mean," Eli said.

"Oh, you know."

Eli smiled and drank his coffee.

A little later, after he had cleaned up, Eli walked over to Cali's. It was a cloudy day. The air was heavy with heat and the threat of rain. To the west the clouds were darker. A storm was coming, it wouldn't be too much longer now, Eli thought.

That was alright. Actually, better than alright. A summer storm provided the perfect excuse to stay inside. Much as he loved those long, hot, summer days, a storm offered a different type of beauty. There was something cozy about being huddled inside under a blanket while the storm raged outside.

He knocked on the door and waited for Cali to come downstairs. She poked her head in the door's window and smiled. Then she unlocked the door and let Eli in.

Her hair was messy and she was wearing an oversized tee-shirt that came halfway down her thighs. The black shirt had the colorful album art of one of her favorite bands. The print was faded, but Eli still recognized what had once been a bright blue and purple image. It was an old shirt. The cotton had thinned and stretched over time, so the fabric now fell loosely over Cali's torso.

She closed and locked the door before she wrapped her arms around Eli.

"I missed you," she said.

"I missed you too."

Then she let go and bounded across the room to the couch.

"Okay, so obviously we are watching movies all day," she said tugging a corner of her shirt. "I'm cozy and this is as much as I'm getting around."

"That's good, I wanted to stay inside today anyway," Eli said.

Cali shot him a playful smile.

"Now, I was thinking old-school horror. We got Frankenstein, The Wolfman and The Mummy," she pointed to the coffee table full of movies. Eli took his shoes off and sat down next to her on the couch.

"Or we can go the sci-fi route and watch the original Planet of the Apes," she said. Eli perused their film options.

"Decisions, decisions," he said. "What do you want more?"

"It's a toss-up, but probably horror."

"Alright. Let's go that route then," Eli said.

"Okay. I already started the popcorn," she said jumping from the couch and running toward the kitchen. "I think one big bowl is enough for right now, don't you?"

Eli followed her to the kitchen and laughed as he watched her pluck a handful of popcorn from the top of the bowl.

"That should be plenty," he said.

He slid his arms around her and rested his chin on her shoulder. Cali fed him a piece of popcorn. Then she spun in his arms so they were facing each other and she kissed him lightly on the neck.

Eli moved his hand up her back and ran his fingers through her hair.

"It's a mess," she said.

"It's perfect," he said gently tugging playfully at her long dark locks.

Cali tilted her head back, her emerald eyes meeting Eli's gaze. She took a piece of popcorn from her hand, balancing it ever so gracefully on the end of her tongue. Her eyes narrowed as a smile crossed her face. Eli leaned a little closer. Cali smiled. The piece of popcorn wavered on the tip of her tongue. Eli leaned closer still. But before he could get nearer, Cali swallowed the popcorn and kissed him gently on the lips.

"Come on. We should go to the living room," Cali said as their lips parted.

"Right. The movie," Eli said taking a step back.

"Yeah. The movie," Cali laughed.

They set up the living room, blankets and pillows spread out along the couch, the curtains closed and a candle lit on the coffee table. After a short discussion, they decided on Frankenstein. Cali popped the movie in the TV and hit play.

Eli sunk into the soft couch. Cali nestled up next to him, her head resting on his shoulder. Eli brushed his face against her hair and breathed deep, taking in her sweet scent. They extended the leg rest on the sofa and reclined the seat until it was nearly flat. Cali cuddled closer, moving her head from Eli's shoulder to his chest and resting her hand on his thigh.

"Are you comfortable?" she asked.

"Yeah, this is perfect," he said.

Cali moved her hand up his thigh.

"You still comfortable?" she asked.

"Even more so," he said.

Cali giggled and pulled the blanket over them. And time drifted away. Minutes and hours slipped by.

They had fallen into a comfortable afternoon nap when the sound of the doorknob startled them both awake. Cali's eyes grew wide. She slid out from under the blanket and motioned for Eli to stay quiet. Cali started across the living room, but the door was already open and in walked her father.

"Dad! You're home early," Cali said as she stepped into the doorway and gave him a hug.

"Yea. The rain didn't help matters. So, we wrapped up early," he said. "What are you up to?"

Before she could answer, he glanced at the couch where Eli was still seated. Eli felt the blood rush to his face. Cali's father raised his eyebrows in surprise, a sneer pulled at the corner of his lips.

"Eli! What are you doing here?" he asked.

"Hello Mr. Anderson," Eli said. His throat was tight and his tongue dry.

Cali's father turned to his daughter.

"Cali," he said as his eyes narrowed and he ran his hand over his chin.

"We were just watching a movie," she said.

"Is that so?" Mr. Anderson nodded as he looked over the room. "Funny, but I'm pretty sure you aren't supposed to have anyone over while your mother and I are gone."

"We were just watching a movie," Cali said.

"Mhm," Mr. Anderson shook his head as he stepped into the living room. "Eli, you can leave."

Eli pulled the blanket off his lap. His face was hot and he felt the blood pounding in his temples. He slipped into his shoes and walked across the living room, head down, trying to avoid eye contact.

"Dad, come on. I'm sixteen, what's the big deal if I spend time with my boyfriend?" Cali asked.

"Boyfriend?"

Mr. Anderson reached out and stopped Eli as he tried to walk past.

"Cali, I don't care if you are 16, 18 or 29, if you are living in my house you will follow my rules," Mr. Anderson said without taking his hand from Eli's shoulder. "And as for you, count this as your warning. I don't want to catch you here alone with my daughter again."

Eli raised his head and caught the look in Mr. Anderson's eyes. Eli knew he should just nod and say what Cali's father wanted to hear, but something inside him bubbled to the surface and before he could stop himself the words rolled off his tongue.

"Well, since you're here now, is it alright if I stay?" he said. Whatever power had compelled him to speak was quickly replaced with regret.

Eli saw the muscles in Mr. Anderson's neck tighten.

"Get out," Mr. Anderson said.

Eli turned and mouthed the words "I'm sorry" to Cali. She shook her head.

Eli stepped outside and felt his heart sink. It had been such a perfect day. But now, it was over, hours before it should be. He glanced down, his fist was clenched. He took a deep breath and let it out slowly, relaxing the muscles in his hand as he exhaled. He took another breath.

Then he walked down the steps to the sidewalk. He glanced back. Cali was in the window. Eli gave a small wave and started off down the street. Cali waved and then disappeared from view.

A quick wave goodbye, that was the last they would see each other this day. Maybe if he kept his mouth shut, he thought. No, it probably didn't matter. Eli wasn't supposed to be there while Cali's parents were at work. They were bound to get caught eventually. It was probably better that they were just watching movies today. He could only imagine how much worse it could have been if Cali's father had walked in while they were doing something else. Still, it felt like hours of their day had been stolen.

Eli wandered aimlessly. He didn't have anything to do or anywhere to be. Most days that was a blessing. It meant he could spend the day strolling around town with Cali. Or maybe, like today, they would stay inside and watch movies. Or else, they would go down to the river and skip rocks. Either way, the days were theirs. Except now, with Cali stuck at home and Eli not allowed to be there, he felt lost.

He kicked a rock and watched it tumble down the wet sidewalk, over the curb and down the gutter. The heavy rain had passed. There was just a light mist in the air now. The darkest clouds had all moved east. Though the sky was still overcast, there probably wouldn't be any more rain today. Not that it mattered much now.

Eli walked on, past the only gas station in town. Neon lights flashed in the windows. A young couple probably a few years older than Eli walked out with sodas. They were laughing as they got into a car parked at one of the gas pumps. Eli watched as they kissed and then sped off for who-knows-where.

I want that, Eli thought. The ability to just get away from everything and everyone. To get lost with Cali on some back road somewhere. To lose all thought of time and just go, anywhere.

He just needed a car and money, lots of money.

Eli walked into the storefront. A Help Wanted sign was taped to the counter next to the register. A woman sat behind the counter reading.

"Are you hiring?" Eli asked as he stepped up to the counter.

The woman lifted her head from her book. She looked Eli up and down. Then shook her head and went back to reading.

"But what about this Help Wanted sign?" he asked.

"So, you can read," the woman said putting down her book.

"Well yea," Eli said.

"Then why'd ya ask if we were hiring?" she asked.

"I don't know, I was just trying to get an application."

"You shoulda just asked for an application."

"Can I have an application then?"

The woman reached under the counter and pulled out a folder marked new hires.

"Just fill out the front, the back is for the store manager to fill out," she said handing Eli the paper and a pen.

Eli took the paper and sat at an empty booth. It didn't take long to fill out the form. He had no previous work experience; this was actually the first application he had ever filled out. When he was done, he gave the paper back to the woman at the counter. She shoved the application in a drawer and said to stop back in if he didn't hear anything in a couple days. Eli thanked her and headed back outside.

With nothing left to do and now bored of walking the streets, Eli returned home. His grandma was in front of the TV with another cup of coffee. Eli didn't bother to ask how much she had gone through since this morning.

He plopped down on the couch beside her and half-heartedly watched whatever she had on. At first it was a game show, then a soap opera, and then another game show. Before he knew it, a few hours had passed. Beams of light stretched across the living room floor as the sun emerged from behind the clouds. It hovered over the horizon and cast its rays through an open window. The day was wasting away.

Eli's stomach growled. He stood and stretched deep.

His grandmother was half-awake in her spot on the couch. Eli decided not to rouse her. He went to the kitchen, rummaged through the cupboard until he found some cherry toaster pastries. He didn't bother to warm them. As he munched the dry tarts, he glanced around the room. There was no sign of Eric. Maybe he left? Eli shrugged his shoulders. What did it matter? Grandma would always let Eric stay here, even if Eli protested. He might as well just get used to his brother being here.

He finished his snack and went back out to the living room. The TV was turned to some celebrity game show and his grandmother was fully asleep now. So, Eli let her be and went up to his room.

There was nothing to do and nothing he wanted to do. If anything, he just wanted to go through the motions of something. Not actual work, not actually doing anything, just moving his body while his mind wandered. There was a basketball in the corner. He didn't want to walk to the park though. Instead, he rummaged under his bed until he found a notebook. He flipped to the back page and then he pulled a set of sketch pencils from beneath his bed stand and started to draw.

He started with a light grey pencil and made a basic oval shape. Then he added some lines along the top of the oval, wavy and long, they would become hair as the drawing took shape. As he moved to the next pencil he drew eyes and lips, still light, but just a shade darker. He continued to add detail as he worked his way through the set of pencils, until he was finally finished.

He sighed and looked over the picture. It was too crisp, clean. The shades of grey added the emphasis he wanted, but the lines were too sharp. He took his index finger and ran it along one of the lines. It smudged slightly. That was a little better, he thought. He traced the lines of Cali's face. He brushed his finger along her jaw and through her hair. He lightly darkened her cheeks to more accurately reflect her skin tone. But he didn't touch her eyes, he left them sharp. When he was finished he held the notepad back and looked at his work. Not bad, he thought. He really was happy with the eyes. The detail really popped against the rest of the drawing. It wasn't perfect yet, but he was getting better. Always improving.

He glanced at his bed stand alarm clock. It was going on 10 p.m. He looked out the window at the dark street.

Just then he heard something outside, just a quiet noise. Maybe an animal? He heard it again, a little clearer this time, someone was talking. He leaned into the window frame, his face pressed against the screen, but he didn't see anything in the dark. Then, there was a flash of light from just below his window. The light flickered, then went out. Eli blinked and turned his eyes to the spot where the light had come from.

There was a shadow, someone was standing there. He squinted. The light flashed again and Eli saw her clearly. Cali was there, waving for him to come down.

A smile spread across his face. He tucked his notebook back under his bed and put his pencils away quickly. Then he hurried down the stairs and through the living room.

Cali met him at the front steps.

"What are you doing?" he asked, taking her in his arms and squeezing her tight.

"We were supposed to hang out today," she said. "I'm trying to make up for lost time."

"Your dad is going to kill you if he finds out," Eli said.

"Then we won't let him find out," she said.

She took his hand and they started off toward the end of the street where the river bank ran. They climbed the little hill and looked out at the water.

"It's beautiful at night isn't it?" Cali said, as she slipped beneath Eli's arm and stepped closer to hug him.

The water reflected the starlight from above, dark ripples dancing in the light of billion-year-old stars.

Eli pressed his lips to Cali's head.

"Let's walk," he whispered.

Cali took his hand and they strolled along the riverbank heading out of town. The river curved gently beside them. Up ahead, the bridge, under which they had skipped rocks yesterday, crossed over the river. Before they got to the bridge, they stopped and found a comfortable spot to rest on the hillside.

Cali leaned back, resting her head on a soft tussock. Eli laid beside her, the earth bending beneath him like a light billowy cushion. The ground was damp. The wild grass grew tall, golden seeds frayed loosely at the top of each shoot and swayed like white feathers in the wind. Bending to and fro in the mild night air, the grass was like a curtain shielding the teens from the rest of the world. Crickets chirped nearby and down by the river frogs called to one another. Eli breathed deep, enjoying the sweet scent of grass and the cool fresh air of the river.

"What are you thinking?" he asked.

"Time," Cali said.

"Time," Eli repeated. The word seemed to waver on the end of his tongue before dissipating in the ether.

"Yea," Cali said. "I was thinking about earlier. How we lost time earlier, a whole afternoon together. But now we have this. If we hadn't lost time earlier we might not be here now. And I feel like this moment is special. It feels good to be out here, with no one else, but the two of us. It feels like right now, there is no time, this is endless. Does that make sense?"

Eli found Cali's hand next to his and brushed his fingertips over her soft palm.

"Yea, it does. It's kinda like things happen how they are supposed to and you don't even realize it at the time," Eli paused and thought, then continued. "It's like later, when you look back that's when you see it. Everything seems to make more sense in the future. But even if you know that, it doesn't make it easier in the moment. I was mad earlier. It felt like we lost the whole day. But I think you're right, if your dad hadn't come home early we might not be out here right now."

"It's crazy, right? Like one thing leads to another and there are affects you don't even know of yet," Cali said.

Eli smiled and rolled onto his side so he was facing Cali. She turned to him, her green eyes shining bright in the dark. Eli brushed a lock of hair out from in front of her face and leaned closer.

"If I kiss you on the cheek like this," Eli said, as he lightly touched her cheek with his lips. "What are the effects?"

Cali smiled and closed her eyes.

"Where should I begin?" she asked.

Eli laughed. Cali's fingers wove into his hair. She pressed her lips to his. They tasted the sweetness of one another.

They rolled, never close enough, but always pushing, feeling, trying to get closer. They turned and Eli gazed down at Cali, her eyes were big and her pupils pulsed gently taking in what light there was. Her hands were wrapped around Eli's waist, she slid one hand under his shirt and ran her fingers along his lower back. Then she eased the shirt up over his shoulders. Eli shrugged it off the rest of the way and tossed it to the side.

Cali ran her hand over his shoulder. The air was cool against his skin. Cali felt his chest and then roamed to his back again.

Eli leaned closer, the fabric of Cali's shirt was soft against his bare chest. Beneath him, he felt her heart beat against his as he leaned closer still and pressed his lips to the soft part of her neck. Cali sighed.

The tender sounds of love drifted through the air and became one with the night, like the cool rush of wind against the grass or the gentle splash of water over rocks.

The air was warm and they could have comfortably stayed out all night, but eventually, they decided to head home.

Cali stood in front of the door and held Eli's hands in her own.

"Promise me something," she said.

"Anything."

"Promise me that we will always have this. This time, where it's just you and me and nothing else matters," she said.

"This is all I want," Eli said.

Cali blinked, the starlight reflecting in her eyes, glistening bright as a tear formed in the corner. She turned her face away, but Eli saw a tear run down her cheek.

He wrapped his arms around her and Cali buried her face in his chest. She shook quietly, her tears wetting the front of Eli's shirt. He held her close, his hand resting on her shoulder and his head bowed down to touch the top of hers.

When she lifted her head, tears clung to the corners of her eyes. Eli used his shirt to dab them dry. Cali smiled shyly.

"I'm sorry," she said.

"There's nothing to be sorry about," Eli said.

Cali ran her hand through her hair, brushing it to the side and exhaled softly.

"I guess, I just think about us and I worry. Like I love what we have right now, this is perfect, but what's going to happen in another year when we are both out of school?"

Eli nodded. He knew her fear. He felt it too. Squeezing her hands, he smiled.

"I'll always be here for you. No matter what the future holds," he said.

Cali smiled. Then, leaning forward on her tiptoes she kissed him on the lips.

She stepped back, still holding Eli's hands.

"I wish tonight didn't have to end," Cali said.

"Someday, it will be like that," Eli said. "We won't have to leave."

"I like that idea."

"Me too, I can't wait for that day."

Cali stepped forward again, placed her hands on Eli's chest, and rocked forward onto her toes for their last kiss goodnight. Eli clasped his hands together in the small of her back. And for that moment, they were one.

"I love you, Eli," Cali said softly as they separated.

"I love you."

With that, Cali quietly stepped inside and closed the door behind her so that it didn't make a sound.

Chapter 5

When Eli returned home, the house was quiet. He eased his way up the stairs and to his room, careful not to wake his grandmother or Eric, if he was even home. He kicked his shoes to the side and threw his shirt on the floor as he fell into bed. It was late, or early, depending how you looked at it. He was ready for sleep.

Eli replayed the night's excursion in his mind. Cali's lips, the cool grass beneath them, the night had been more than he could have hoped for. Slowly the memories turned to dream, reality mingled with fantasy.

Eli brushed his hand over Cali's cheeks, she smiled, he felt the corner of her lips curl beneath his fingertips. She closed her eyes and sunk deeper in the grass. Eli kissed her once more on the lips and lay down beside her. The night was tranquil, he could hear her breathing softly beside him. Above, the moon hovered behind a layer of purplish gray clouds.

But then, darker, heavier clouds disturbed the peace. They raced across the sky, quickly overtaking the lighter cirrus clouds and fully blanketed the moon. Eli's eyes adjusted to the darkness. He glanced over at Cali. Her breathing had slowed. She was asleep.

Eli watched, and noticed her head nob ever so slightly as she slipped further into the world of dreams. Her breathing was shallow, barely noticeable. Eli watched and for a moment it seemed like maybe she had stopped breathing. He counted, one, two, three, four. The seconds slipped past. His heart skipped a beat.

What if?

He shook the image from his mind. And then he saw Cali's chest rise, she was alive. He breathed a sigh of relief, but something frightful lingered. In her rest, Cali seemed like Sleeping Beauty, caught between the living and the dead, endlessly waiting. Was she like the fairy tale, had she pricked her finger? Had a spindle caused this endless sleep, or was there something else?

Life balanced so precariously to death, it didn't take much to fall one way or the other. Sleep was just a little death anyway. And living? Well, that was a dream for the dead.

In the dark, Eli's thoughts seemed to manifest a life of their own. Cali's skin took on a grayish tint. Was it the light of the moon? Eli turned, the night sun was still hidden behind the clouds. Shifting his gaze back to Cali, he saw a pale ghost beside him, her skin so ashen white it seemed translucent. Eli reached over and placed his hand on her shoulder. But as he did so, his fingers accidently brushed her neck. A chill raced through his hand and up his arm. She was freezing.

Eli propped himself on his elbow and nudged her shoulder.

"Cali, wake up," he said.

She didn't respond.

"Cali?"

He shook her, hoping for something, some movement, but still nothing. Dark thoughts jumped to the front of his mind. She was dead. Cali was dead.

His heart raced, his pulse pounding in his ears.

"Cali!" he yelled shaking her. Cali's lifeless body rocked to the side and her mouth drooped open.

"Cali! Cali!"

Tears welled in the corners of his eyes and streaked down his cheeks in hot streams. He wiped them away, his vision blurred. This wasn't right. This couldn't be happening. She couldn't be dead. She wasn't dead. No, she needed help. He could save her.

He would have to carry her. They needed to get back to town, then they could find help. He clambered to his knees and turned her lifeless body to him. He positioned his arm underneath her shoulders and lifted her. But just then, he was startled by the rustling of grass nearby.

Eli turned his eyes toward the sound. It was too dark to see much, but there just a few feet away hunkered down in the grass he thought he saw the shape of a person. For a moment, neither Eli nor the figure moved. Then, it spoke to him, it's voice rough and gravely.

"What have you done?" it said.

Eli shook his head and pulled Cali closer to him. "She needs help," he said.

"What have you done to my daughter?"

The figure stepped forward, growing taller and looming above Eli and Cali. The shadow no longer a mystery, Eli saw the details of Cali's father come into focus as he stepped closer. His face contorted in rage, his eyes like two red flames glaring down at Eli.

"What have you done!" he screamed.

Eli struggled to his feet, Cali's body limp in his arms.

"You killed her!" Cali's father bellowed. "You did this!"

Then, he lunged forward. His fingers clawed at Eli's face before finding their way to his throat. Eli stumbled backward. Cali slipped from his arms, and crashed to the ground, disappearing in the dark. Her father overpowered Eli. They fell. The man's weight crushed and pinned him to the ground. Eli struggling for breath as the older, stronger man throttled him.

"I'll kill you! I'll kill you!" Cali's father cried, his voice shrill in Eli's ears.

Eli twisted his arm free and pried the older man's hand from his throat. Once loose from his grasp, Eli pushed himself to the side and slipped out of reach. He clambered to his hands and knees, but lost his balance and tumbled down the hillside and splashed into the river below. Cali's father was right there behind him, trudging his way through the grass and out into the stream. Eli tried to get his feet under him, but Cali's father moved faster and was already on top of him again. With a quick shove, he knocked Eli off balance. Eli fell hard on the slick river rocks, dashing the back of his head on a stone. Blood swirled through the water.

Cali's father rushed forward and dove upon the teenager. He trapped Eli on the river bottom and held him fast.

The rocks dug into Eli's back. He struggled to break free. But there was no escape this time. Cali's father was stronger and heavier and now had a firm hold of Eli. There was little Eli could do, he felt himself drifting. He opened his mouth and tried to scream. Water filled his lungs. Then everything turned gray.

Eli lurched awake. He sat upright in bed gasping for breath. Sweat dripped from his forehead. His head buzzed with the sound of Cali's father yelling in his ears. He took deep breaths to steady his nerves. His hands went to his throat. Relief passed over him as he felt his neck. It was just a dream. He sighed and sunk back into his pillow and let his heart rate normalize.

The first glint of morning was just starting to peak though the window. He knew he wouldn't get back to sleep, so he climbed out of bed, put on a fresh shirt and glanced in the mirror. His hair was a mess. Instead of combing it, he threw on a hat that was sitting on his dresser and then made his way downstairs.

Eric was sitting on the couch drinking a cup of coffee. The whiskey bottle was on the floor at his feet. Behind the warm smell of coffee, Eli recognized the tangy alcohol odor that clung to his brother.

"Late night?" Eric asked as Eli walked past.

Eli didn't answer and instead went to the doorway that led to the kitchen. He expected to see his grandma at the table with her morning coffee, but the kitchen was empty.

"Where's grandma?" Eli asked.

"Hell, if I know," Eric said.

"Was she here when you got up?"

"I don't keep tabs on her," Eric said. "She probably went to the store."

Eli went to the front door and looked outside, his grandma's car was still out front.

"She would have drove," Eli said.

"Then she's probably just sleeping in. She's an old woman, she can sleep in if she wants," Eric said.

"Yeah," Eli sat down on the other end of the couch, away from Eric.

His head was still spinning from his dream. He ran his hand along his neck, trying to shake the lingering feeling.

"You snuck out last night," Eric prodded.

"Where were you?" Eli asked.

"I was here," Eric said.

"No. I would have seen you," Eli said.

"It don't matter. What'd ya do? Go see a girl?"

Eli glanced at his brother and shook his head.

"Shut up," he said.

"Eli. Little baby Eli sneaking out to see his girlfriend."

"Drop it."

"What? Eli's too shy? Doesn't want to kiss and tell? Poor baby Eli. Or maybe he can't get any. That's it isn't it? Poor baby Eli, can't get laid," Eric teased.

"Shut up. At least I'm not out knocking up girls I don't even know," Eli said.

"Oh, I know them. There's just so many it's hard to keep them all straight."

"I bet. I'm sure they're just beating down the door to get to you," Eli said.

"It ain't easy bein' easy," Eric said.

"Screw off," Eli said as he got up and went to the front door again. "If you see grandma tell her I'll be back later."

"What leaving already? Why don't ya wanna talk with me Eli?" Eric asked.

"Just tell her I'll be back," Eli said.

"Come on, why don't ya stay. You can have a drink with me," Eric said nudging the whiskey bottle with his foot.

Eli shook his head then marched out to the kitchen. He found a scrap of paper on the counter and left a note for his grandma. He stuck it under the napkin holder on the table.

Then, he went back through the living room and didn't say a word to Eric before going outside.

His fist was clenched in a ball, his jaw set firm. He ground his teeth as he started walking. He couldn't stay in that house another minute. Not with Eric there. As he walked he felt his blood begin to cool and after a few minutes he could actually think straight. He put his hands in his pocket and continued on down the road onto Main Street to the other end of town.

The houses seemed to grow larger as he walked down Main Street. Big shinning windows looked out at the road like toothy smiles. Happy families eating their perfect breakfasts sat behind those windows, Eli thought. Perfect families without alcoholic brothers and absent parents.

His thoughts drifted.

How far gone was normal? Whiskey with breakfast, was that too far? What sort of problems lay hidden behind these smiling windows? Did they have the same problems, were they just better at hiding them? How many people were living a lie, pretending it was all okay? Hiding their vices behind a smile and a well-manicured lawn. That was the measure of success, not that you didn't have problems, but how well could you hide them. With enough money, you could buy a world of lies, but as long as you looked happy who would ever know?

That was the American Dream, Eli thought. Live the lie. Your happy life, your happy lie. He needed to get out of this town, the hopelessness was endemic. He wasn't going to stay here and live the same dismal life as everyone else. Not if he could help it.

He would leave with Cali and they would go someplace far away from all of this, the ocean. A beach or a rocky coast up north, somewhere different, away from here. Someplace beautiful, where they wouldn't have to think about this town or anyone in it again. It would all just be a memory, like a bad dream.

His thoughts went back to last night's dream. Cali's lifeless eyes stared back at him. He shivered.

He wanted to talk to her and rid himself of the memory of that dream.

Eli glanced at the sky. The sun was over the horizon but hidden by a layer of early morning clouds. Cali's parents should be gone for work, or leaving soon he thought.

So, Eli made his way toward Cali's, hoping she would be awake.

Chapter 6

Eli knocked on the door. He was met with silence. He waited a minute before knocking a second time. If she didn't answer he would leave and come back later. He didn't want to wake her.

But just then he heard movement upstairs. Then the soft patter of Cali's bare feet coming down the steps. She poked her head in the window and gave Eli a warm smile before opening the door and inviting him in.

"You're up early," she said. She hadn't been up long, Eli thought. She was still in her pajamas, a baggy pair of sweatpants and an oversized t-shirt.

"Yea, I couldn't sleep anymore," he said.

"I see that," Cali said. She snatched Eli's hat off his head and threw it on the couch. "You look better without this, even if you still have bedhead."

Eli smiled.

"Want some coffee?" Cali asked as she made her way to the kitchen.

Eli thought of Eric drinking coffee and the bottle of whiskey at his feet.

"No, I think I'll be alright," he said.

"I'm making some," Cali said. "I'll make enough if you change your mind."

She started filling the pot with water.

"Last night was fun," she said, flashing Eli a quick smile. She scooped the coffee grounds into the basket and closed the lid on the coffee maker. It gurgled to life.

"Yea it was," Eli said. "It was nice to be alone."

"I know," she agreed. "The days go by too fast. It's like they are already over before they even begin."

She turned and watched the coffee trickle into the pot.

"Then there are days when my parents get home early and the little bit of time we have is stolen," she said.

"Do you think they will be okay with us?" Eli asked.

"I don't know," she said. She leaned back against the counter and turned her attention back to Eli. The coffee percolated behind her. The warm aroma wafting through the room made Eli start to reconsider whether he wanted a cup.

"I want to say yea," Cali said. "Like eventually, they are just going to have to come to terms with us being together. That's not something that's going to change. But at the same time, it's like they don't even want to accept the fact that we're together. They still think of me like I'm still their 10-year old daughter who is waiting for their approval for everything."

"I guess we just have to make the most of the time we've got," Eli said. "It'll be different eventually."

"It just sucks," she said.

Their conversation continued for some time until the coffee finished brewing. Then, they migrated to the bedroom. Cali tip-toed up the stairs, careful not to spill a drop from her mug. Eli followed close behind with his own mug.

They set their coffees on the bed stand as they got comfortable under an oversized blanket. Once cozy, they sipped their drinks and talked. Conversation weaved seamlessly from one topic to another with barely a pause.

They finished their drinks long before the conversation ended. They set their mugs to the side and drew close together.

Cali kissed Eli along the neck. Her breath tickled his skin and caused the hair on his arm to rise as a shiver passed through him. He turned and found her lips.

Eli's hand rested on Cali's leg as they kissed. Cali squeezed his hand and guided him up the length of her thigh.

Her feet were entwined with his. Her toes traced circles along the top of his feet. Eli felt the long muscles of her thigh move beneath his hand.

They kissed and sank deeper into the pillows, all the while focusing more attention to the game their hands played. Eli moved his palm up Cali's thigh. Cali moved closer, her hand moving up Eli's leg and hip. She continued exploring, her fingers glided along the smooth skin of his side before toying with his belt. Eli's heart was racing, his mind a flurry of thoughts.

Cali moved her leg and Eli eased his hand up her soft cotton sweats to the elastic band along her waist. Then, as his fingers moved over her hip, he felt the soft transition of fabric. The elastic banding of her sweatpants gave way to a cool silky material beneath.

Cali took Eli's lower lip in her teeth and tugged playfully, pulling him closer. Eli inched his fingers over her hip and Cali responded with another tug on his lip. Meanwhile, her fingers played with the button on his jeans. Cali's chest was pressed tight to Eli's and as they kissed, he felt her heartbeat quicken.

Just then there was a loud pounding from downstairs. Eli and Cali both jumped. The air caught in Eli's lungs and for a moment they stared at each other, eyes wide. Then Cali's eyebrows narrowed as she listened for something more. Eli strained his ears too. He heard someone speaking, then someone knocked on the door again. This time louder and harder.

"It's not my dad," Cali said.

"Should we answer it?" Eli asked.

Cali looked at him, her big eyes reading his face.

"Let's go down to the bottom of the stairs and see if we can hear better. I heard a voice," she said.

"Me too, I couldn't hear what they said though."

Cali nodded.

They left the comforts of Cali's room and walked quietly downstairs. At the bottom step they stopped and leaned against the railing, listening as best they could.

Someone was definitely outside talking. From the tone of the person's voice, it sounded like a man. Most of what he said was still unintelligible though, mostly.

"Did he just say your name?" Cali asked.

There came another series of knocks and then the man on the porch hollered so there was no mistaking it.

"For Christ sakes Eli, open the damn door. It's me!" Eli's brother yelled from outside.

"What the hell?" Eli leaped down the stairs and across the living room to the front door. Cali hurried beside him. Eli threw open the door.

"Eric? What the hell are you doing here?" Eli asked.

"It's grandma Eli, I don't know what to do," Eric cried.

"Wait. Hold on. What's going on?"

"Grandma, she won't move. I can't get her out of bed, she is just shaking," Eric said.

"How long has she been like this? Did you call 9-1-1?" Eli said as he hurried and grabbed his shoes and hat. He stumbled out the door. Cali was right beside him. She had slipped into a pair of sneakers. She closed the door as they ran down the steps.

"I didn't know what to do. I didn't call anyone. Cause. . ." Eric started.

"Cause you're drunk!" Eli yelled.

"I didn't know. I didn't know what to do Eli," Eric sputtered. Tears tumbled down his face.

"Shut up," Eli said. "We need to hurry."

The three of them rushed down the street, past the run-down homes and drunken stares of neighbors. Eli bounded up the stairs in two steps and raced through the living room and upstairs to his grandma's room. There in the dark, his grandma lay quietly in bed. The covers were pulled up to her shoulders, and she appeared motionless beneath. Eli walked slowed to the side of the bed. Behind him he heard Eric in the doorway. Eli glanced back. Eric was standing alone. Cali must be downstairs, Eli thought.

He turned back to his grandma.

"Hey," he said as he knelt beside the bed. "Grandma, can you hear me?"

He reached out and placed his hand upon her forehead, she was warm. He watched the covers rise and fall slightly. Good, he thought. She's not dead.

He turned to Eric.

"Call 9-1-1," he said.

"Is she okay?"

"I don't know," Eli said.

Eric nodded and left the room. Eli heard him shuffle downstairs to make the call. He glanced back at his grandmother and placed a hand on her shoulder.

"You're gonna be alright," he said.

She sighed and turned her head just a little on the pillow.

"It's going to be alright," he said again.

The ambulance arrived about fifteen minutes later. They loaded the elderly woman onto a transport gurney and then into the van. The driver and a local police officer talked with Eli and Eric. Cali waited in the kitchen sipping a cup of coffee so as not to intrude on a delicate family situation. She offered to leave, but Eli asked her to stay. So now she waited.

As they loaded Eli's grandmother into the van the driver told Eli who to call to check on her. Eli and Eric thanked the medical team and watched as the van drove off, flashing red lights fading in the distance.

"I'm sorry, Eli," Eric said resting his hand on his brother's shoulder.

Eli laughed and shook his head.

"You're sorry. That's great. At least there's that. You're sorry," Eli said as he took a step away from Eric.

"What do you want me to say?"

"I don't expect or want anything from you," Eli said.

"Then what? What am I supposed to do?"

"I don't care what you do. You still have a half bottle of whiskey on the floor. You better finish that," Eli said. "Just leave me the hell alone."

"Eli. . ." Eric started. Eli cut him off.

"No. I don't want to hear your voice, whining and crying. Poor Eric. I don't want to hear about your problems. Grandma could have died today, hell she could still die. I don't know. But your first reaction wasn't to call 9-1-1? Anyone with half a brain would have called for an ambulance as soon as they saw her. How drunk were you? How drunk are you all the time? How can you even function?"

"Eli I was scared. I'm sorry," Eric sobbed, tears streaming down his face. "I screwed up, okay? I'm sorry."

"Shut up. Just go drink your whiskey and leave me alone."

Eli left his brother standing in the doorway. He went to the kitchen and took Cali's hand.

"Come on, let's get out of here," he said.

"Eli. What did the EMTs say?" she asked.

"I'll tell you later, come on."

They left the kitchen and headed for the front door.

Eric was sitting in the recliner. The bottle of whiskey on the floor next to him. He didn't look up as Eli and Cali passed. Eli grabbed his grandmother's keys off the hook by the door as they stepped outside.

"Let's go for a drive," he said.

"Eli are you sure that's a good idea?"

He stopped and looked at Cali. His eyes were dark and his jaw set. Then he smiled.

"It's up to you. I'm going for a drive, I just want to clear my head."

Cali squeezed his hand.

"Okay, let's go," she said.

Chapter 7

It was warm out, even though the sun was still hidden behind a thick layer of gray clouds. Cali had her window down and the breeze was blowing through her hair. Eli glanced over and smiled to himself. Her eyes were closed and a smiled formed at the corner of her lips.

Eli felt somewhat better. It had taken a bit, but once they got out of town it was like a weight had lifted from his shoulders.

He turned left onto a dirt road. A cloud of dust kicked up behind them as they cruised along. The road was fairly smooth, with not too many pot holes to be found. A fresh layer of loose gravel snapped and popped under the car's tires as they rolled along. The car drifted on the stones, but as long as they didn't go too fast it wasn't bad.

Up ahead tall pines bordered the road on either side. Though the sun was hidden, the pines still seemed to cast long shadows. A thick canopy of green blotted out much of the sky. The branches overhead provided natural isolation.

"When are you going to take your driver's test?" Eli asked.

Cali opened her eyes and turned to him. Her bright green gaze soft and warm.

"I'm not in a hurry," she said. "You can drive me around."

"Oh, so I'm just your chauffer?" Eli laughed.

"Well, not just my chauffer," Cali said as she placed her hand on his thigh.

Eli took her hand in his.

"Seriously though, you've had your permit for a bit now. When can you take your test?"

"September. I want to practice more though, I don't get to drive enough with my parents. It's just uptown or maybe a trip to the mall on the weekend," Cali said. "How long did it take you to feel comfortable?"

"I don't know, grandma made it easy," Eli said. "She made me get my license as soon as I could. She wanted me to be able to drive her around. I don't remember ever feeling awkward. I think because she wanted me to be comfortable, so she really tried to encourage me. Does that make sense?"

"Yeah it does. My mom gets so uptight when I drive, I'm always worried I'm going to do something wrong and my Dad is worse. He is like correcting everything I do. It feels like I can't do anything right," Cali said.

Eli turned to her. Then he put the car in neutral and coasted to a stop along the side of the road.

"Do you want to practice?" he asked.

"Right now? I don't even have my permit, what if someone sees us? Or what if I wreck your grandma's car?" she said. "Plus, I've never driven standard."

Eli looked around. Then he opened his door and stepped outside. He walked around the front of the car and opened Cali's door.

"There is no one around. Besides, this road goes on for miles with no traffic. You can just drive. I'll teach you how to drive stick."

"But what if I hit something and ruin your grandma's car?" Cali asked, even though she was already taking off her seatbelt and stepping outside.

"Don't worry, you won't. Just take it slow, we aren't in a hurry," he said.

Cali walked around to the driver's side and got in. Eli settled into the passenger seat and watched as Cali adjusted the mirrors and moved the seat closer to the wheel. She double checked the mirrors and turned to Eli, a big smile on her face.

"Ready?" Eli asked.

She nodded.

"Alright, let's go," he said.

Cali looked at him and waited.

"Step on the clutch with you left foot. It's the third pedal over. Yep, step all the way down."

Cali stepped on the clutch.

"Okay, you can take your foot off the clutch for a minute."

She lifted her foot and waited expectantly.

"Okay, now put your hand on the shifter," he said.

With her hand on the stick, Eli guided her through the gears showing her where she would move the stick when she shifted.

"Okay now first gear is hardest, but once you get moving it's not too bad. So, step on the clutch and put it in first, but don't let your foot off the clutch yet."

"What if I have to stop?" she asked.

"What do you mean, you just step on the brake," he said.

"But won't that make it stall out?"

"Oh, yea. So, when you stop just step on both, the clutch and the brake," he said.

"Then I won't stall?"

"No, not if you step on the clutch."

"Okay," Cali said. "So, now what?"

"Let's put it in first," he guided her hand on the shifter and slid it into first gear. "So, go ahead and start to let off the clutch."

"But won't that make it stall?" she asked.

"No, you'll see," he said. "Slowly let off the clutch, not all the way, just until you start to feel it grab."

Cali lifted her foot off the clutch slowly. About halfway off the pedal, she stopped and then stepped back on the clutch.

"I think I felt it," she said. "Like there as nothing, then there was pressure."

"Right, good. When you feel that pressure go ahead and slowly step on the gas. As you give it more gas you will want to step off the clutch more."

Cali lifted her foot off the clutch again and just when it started to catch she stepped on the gas. The engine revved and they sputtered forward. The car jerked and Cali lifted her foot off the clutch and stomped on the gas. The car jumped forward. The tachometer shot past 6000 rpms and went into the red. Cali pulled her foot off the gas. The rpm gauge dropped back down below 1000 and the car puttered to a crawl before stalling.

"It's alright," Eli said. "Let's try again. Try to be smoother when you let off the clutch and don't step so hard on the gas."

"Okay," she said nodding her head. She stared at the dashboard for a moment without moving. Eli watched her, assessing her emotions. Then he caught a look in her eyes. There was a steady determination to

her gaze. Eventually she nodded her head, her mind made up.

"Okay, let's do it."

"Step on the clutch and turn the key," Eli instructed.

Cali did and the car came to life.

"Alright, let's try again, nice and easy this time," Eli said.

Cali lifted her foot off the clutch and as the engine started to catch she stepped on the gas.

"Good, just like that," Eli said.

The car started to move forward and Cali lifted her foot off the clutch and gave it more gas. The car jumped a little. Cali was careful not to step too hard on the gas this time though and they slowly started off down the road.

"Perfect! Good job," Eli said. "Now you are going to want to shift into second."

"How do I do that?" Cali asked. Her left hand was gripping the steering wheel, her right hand firmly holding the shifter.

"Okay, take your foot off the gas and step on the clutch again," Eli said. "And slide this down into second gear."

He watched as she moved the shifter into second.

"Now, step off the clutch," he said.

She followed his directions.

"Step on the gas."

She did and the car continued on down the dirt road.

"Great. You are picking it up easy," he said.

"It's what I do," Cali said with a laugh.

They continued to pick up speed. At about 30 miles an hour the rpms started to climb above 3000. The engine whined.

"Third?" Cali asked.

"Yea, same as before," Eli said.

Cali lifted her foot off the gas and the car slowed. Then, she stepped on the clutch and shifted into third. The car lugged slightly as the rpms dropped lower, but Cali stepped on the gas and they picked up speed again.

The dirt road started up a hill. To their left, the trees opened, exposing the valley below. They climbed steadily uphill, the road to their left revealing more of the green pastures below to the west. There was no guardrail blocking their view. Eli breathed a deep sigh as he enjoyed the scenery.

The road twisted round another bend and levelled out as they came to the top of the hill. The trees grew thicker here, cloaking the entire road in shadow.

"There's a spot to pull off up ahead," Eli said pointing to a break in the woods.

"Do I have to shift back to second?" Cali asked.

"No, when we get closer just put it in neutral and we can cruise into the lot."

As they drew near, Cali slid the shifter into the neutral position, jockeying the stick side to side making sure it wasn't in gear. She pressed the brake pedal gradually and guided the car to the side of the road.

"Nice job," Eli said with a smile.

Cali turned to him, her lips curled at the corner.

"Psh, I got this," she said rapping her knuckles on her shoulder and laughing.

Eli leaned across the seat and planted a kiss on her lips. Cali laughed and kissed him back. They separated and Eli fell back in the passenger seat.

He leaned back in the chair. Cali watched him close his eyes, a smile still playing at his lips. He stretched his arms out and then relaxed, resting his head on his interlocked hands. She smiled and kissed him on the forehead.

"I feel better, being here with you," he said.

"Good," Cali said. "It's been a rough morning."

"I just hope she's okay," Eli said.

"She will be."

"I hope so," Eli trailed off, as he opened his eyes and focused his attention out the window. Cali opened her door and stepped outside. Eli gazed out the window for a minute before blinking and deciding to follow Cali.

She was standing beneath a nearby tree. Her head tilted back and her hair falling down below her shoulders as she looked up.

"What do you see?" Eli asked.

"Just a big tree," Cali said. "It's a pretty tree though."

Eli placed his hand on her back and looked up. The tree was enormous. From where they stood a few feet from the base, Eli couldn't see the top. Dense branches of flat, almost featherlike leaves grew thickly high up the tree. Down low, a branch stretched forth only a few feet above the teenagers' heads. Eli reached up and plucked a small twig of dark green leaves. The evergreen needles were soft to the touch yet firm and resilient. Eli turned the branch between his fingers, the fresh earthy scent of the cypress leaf filled his nostrils.

Cali stepped away from the tree and wandered into the woods. Eli followed. They meandered away from the road and into the forest where the trees grew thick. On the brightest days the sun struggled to penetrate the dense canopy above. So, on an overcast day such as this, it was especially dark between the trees.

"Would you build a house with me?" Cali asked as they ventured into the forest.

"If that's what you wanted," Eli said. "You want to stay around here?"

"Maybe. I like the change of seasons," Cali said.

"I like summer. I like the heat and the days seem longer," Eli said.

Cali moved a branch from the base of the a nearby pine tree and sat down. Eli sat next to her. They relaxed against the tree and sat quietly for some time just taking in the sounds of the forest. There was so much to hear. Birds sang for one another, their melodies forming a choir in the branches above. On the forest floor, twigs snapped and dry leaves rustled as critters scurried to and fro. Life was abundant. A slight breeze rolled between the trees bringing with it the strong aroma of pine needles and undergrowth. Eli breathed deep, letting the air sit in his lungs before exhaling.

"Summer is nice," Cali said after a while. "But don't you like the feel of fall? The leaves changing color and that first bite of cold air? I love it."

"I like fall. I like the leaves changing. But summer is still my favorite. It's like you can escape everything for a little while. Like time doesn't even exist in summer."

"I know what you mean," she said. "You would want to stay here though, even if it wasn't summer all the time?"

"Anywhere with you, that's where I want to be," Eli said.

Cali leaned her head on his shoulder.

"I just want to be here," she said.

"Me too," Eli said closing his eyes and leaning his head against hers.

Chapter 8

Afternoon turned to evening. The sun dipped closer to the horizon and bathed the forest in red and gold. Trees turned to dark silhouettes, while a canopy of interlocking evergreen branches loomed overhead.

Darkness crept closer as day gave way to twilight. Eli and Cali decided to head back to the car before daylight was totally gone.

They weaved their way through tall pines and dense underbrush. Clusters of bushes, some with red and purple berries, forced the teens to travel a circuitous route. Light seeping through the branches above increased as they neared the edge of the forest. They hadn't traveled all that far into the wood, but Eli felt it took a lot longer to walk back than it had to walk in.

They reached the road and Eli opened the passenger door for Cali before walking to the driver's side.

He glanced back at the trees. Though he could only see maybe twenty or thirty feet from the road before the trees all blurred together in the dark, he imagined there was a cabin nestled beneath the pines. A long dirt driveway led to the cozy little cottage. A thin wisp of smoke drifted from a chimney into the evening sky. A pair of windows glowed soft orange from the light a fireplace. There, seated comfortably together on a big sofa, Eli and Cali watched the fire dance long into the night until they fell asleep in each other's arms.

He smiled and got in the car.

"What are you thinking?" Cali asked as they started off along the road and back down the hill toward town.

"Just that I love you," he said.

She took his hand and squeezed lightly.

"I love you too," she said.

The setting sun was beautiful, but blinding. The red glare shined through the windshield directly in Eli's eyes. He lowered the visor, but the sun was shining at that perfect angle making it impossible to shield. The glare was annoying, but Eli drove on. He had traveled this road a hundred times and knew all the twists and turns.

About a mile down the narrow road, a tractor trailer down-shifted to make the climb uphill. The engine chugged as the truck pulled up the steep dirt path. A full load of logs rocked side-to-side as the truck bounded up the rough road.

With the sun in his eyes, Eli couldn't see far ahead at all.

Cali put a CD in the radio.

The truck driver took a sip from his thermos. The coffee was lukewarm and just about gone. He spat it out the window and wiped the spittle from his lips. Then he poured the remaining coffee out the window.

The driver's day was almost done. A quick trip over the hill and back. Then he could have a real cup of coffee with his diner at the restaurant.

Eli listened as Cali sang. Her voice smooth and airy. The words flowed off her tongue and seemed to hover in the air.

The sun dipped lower over the horizon. Eli squinted to no avail. The glare was impossible to contend with.

The truck driver reached across the dashboard to set his thermos back in the cupholder. But the thermos slipped from his hand and fell to the floor. He sighed and unbuckled his seatbelt.

Cali stretched her arm out the window, her hand gliding over the air currents as they sped downhill. She closed her eyes.

Eli glanced to his right. Cali leaned back in her chair. The wind tousled her hair. Eli smiled.

The truck driver held the wheel with his left hand as he leaned below the dash to retrieve the thermos. It only took a second to grab the steel canister.

Eli turned his eyes back to the road. Through dazzling rays of light and a cloud of dust, he saw the semi-truck veering across the road. A pale horse coming straight for them.

Eli cranked the steering wheel hard to the right. The car skid over loose rocks. The back tires swerved and jettisoned off the roadway. Eli quickly tried to correct their course, spinning the wheel to the left and slamming on the brakes. There was little he could do though; their momentum was too great. The car careened off the side of the road and down the steep embankment.

Cali was thrown against the door. Her head dashed against the steel frame, opening a cut along her brow and sending blood pouring down her face. Eli was thrown forward and to the right. His knee smashed into the stick shift, he barely registered the pain before the car began to roll.

A sudden weightlessness came over Eli as he was lifted from his seat and thrown to the side. His slammed into the driver's door. Cali crashed into the dashboard, her outstretch arms were little resistance to the force of the impact.

Wearing seatbelts might have saved them, but it was too late for that.

The car toppled over and the crushing weight of the roof caving in sent glass flying through the cabin. As metal yielded beneath the force of the impact, Eli's door was thrust open and he was sent sprawling through the air. He crashed to the ground some distance away and tumbled hard over the dry earth, dust and dirt filled his mouth and nose. Sharp rocks gauged into his skin and course underbrush scratched his face and arms. His leg buckled and snapped beneath him as he rolled to a stop in a tangle of thorn bushes partway down the hill.

The car toppled down the hill and came to a halt some hundred feet below.

Eli was shaking violently as he tried to gather himself. He lifted his head, but struggled to make sense of where he was, everything was spinning.

His heart pounded. His breath came in shallow and ragged gasps.

"Hey!" someone called behind him. "Don't move. I'll be right down."

Eli collapsed face down. He had just enough strength to turn his head so his eyes focused downhill, where the car was obscured in a cloud of dust. He saw the line of destruction where the car had passed. Pieces of metal and glass littered the hillside. Large swaths of underbrush were crushed flat or ripped up by the roots.

As the dust slowly settled, Eli saw the tangled mass of metal. A thin stream of black smoke trickled skyward from the wreckage. Resting upside down, the car was turned with the driver's side facing uphill. The front door on that side was gone, it was lodged in a bush halfway down the hill. Near the front of the car on the downhill side, Eli saw a shadow move. It was Cali, he thought.

He struggled to stay conscious. He had to know she was okay. She had to be. He fought to keep his eyes open. The shadow near the front of the car moved again, Eli was sure that was her. Somehow, she must have been able to get free from the car. Eli smiled. She was okay. That's all that mattered. He closed his eyes.

Someone rolled him onto his back. They slid him onto a gurney. Eli opened his eyes, bright lights flashed in the distance, the sky was dark above.

"Cali," Eli mumbled.

"Watch his leg, it's broken," someone said.

"Lucky he ain't dead," someone else said.

Firm hands took hold of his leg. Pain radiated sharp and deep. Eli screamed.

"Easy, easy. I told you to watch his leg," the first voice said.

"It's okay hun, we got ya. You're gonna be alright," the first voice said to him.

Eli struggled to lift his head and see who was talking. It was no use, everything hurt.

"Just keep still. We got ya," another voice said.

A cool hand touched his forehead. A woman leaned over him, her face slowly came into focus in the red glow of ambulance lights. A sad smile touched her lips. She brushed Eli's hair out of his face.

"You're gonna be alright," she said.

"Cali," Eli said.

"What's he asking?" someone said.

"The girl," the woman leaning over Eli said over her shoulder.

"Look at me hun," the woman said to Eli. "You are gonna be alright."

"Where's Cali?" he asked.

"She's alright," the woman said.

Eli closed his eyes again. Everything was going to be alright.

Chapter 9

Afternoon turned to evening. The sun dipped closer to the horizon and bathed the forest in red and gold. It was dark and quiet beneath the trees where Eli and Cali still sat holding one another.

"Can't we just stay here forever?" Cali asked.

"And put a house right over there," Eli pointed to a spot of woods not far from where they sat.

"Yea, what do you think of a little cabin?" she asked.

"I like it. Something small, but enough for us," he said.

"Right, we don't need a huge place. Just a cabin with a fireplace so we can be warm in the winter," Cali said.

"Mhm," Eli smiled. "I think that's perfect."

"Me too," she wrapped her arms tighter around him. Eli closed his eyes. The intoxicating mixture of Cali's almond scented hair and the pine needled ground eased him to sleep.

When he opened his eyes, he found himself, years older. He couldn't say how old, but enough that there were grey hairs mingled with the brown on his arms. He was working on something. Slabs of wood were strewn about what seemed to be a garage. Sawdust was all over the floor and on his pants and shirt. He tapped his fingers on the arm of a chair where he sat. On the corner of a table was a stack of papers with his handwriting. Another story. This one was good, it told the story he wanted. More truth than fiction. But there was still so much to do, so much to finish, he felt time slipping away. He sighed.

There was something he was forgetting, but he couldn't place it.

He leaned back in his chair. His head resting in the palm of his hand as he leaned on the armrest and tried to remember. It was something important. It wouldn't come to him. Eventually he let it go and got up. His leg ached deep down to the bone. It was going to rain soon. He sighed and walked across the room to the table saw on the opposite wall. His gait was marked by a pronounced limp. That leg had never healed right after the accident he thought. Oh well, not much could be done about it now.

"Eli?" Cali's voice drifted through the doorway from outside.

"I'm here," he said, turning to face the door.

Cali stepped into the garage. Her brown hair was streaked with grey, but her face was still young and beautiful. She wore a long navy-blue dress and a pair of nice white sandals.

"Are you going to get around?" she asked.

"For what?" he asked.

The scene shifted and he was back in the forest. He was alone now.

"Cali," he called.

No answer.

"Cali, where are you?" he called.

He stood and walked deeper into the woods, expecting her to pop out from behind a tree. There was a big pine a little distance ahead. That's where she'll be, he thought. As he got closer, he was careful to mind his step so as not to make any noise. He got right up next to the tree and waited, listening for signs Cali was on the other side. He didn't hear anything, but he knew she had to be there.

He jumped around the side and yelled.

But Cali wasn't there.

A cool breeze passed over his shoulders, almost as if someone sighed right behind him. The hair on his neck stood on end. A twig snapped.

Eli whirled around.

There, skulking before him, stood Eric. His eyes were dark. His mouth twisted in a horrible grin. He stepped closer, his face almost touching Eli's.

"Am I the one you're looking for?" Eric asked. His voice deep and gravelly. It didn't sound like his brother.

Eli stumbled backward.

Eric advanced quickly. Now towering above Eli. He stepped forward, a knife flashed in his hand. Their eyes met.

"She's not here, Eli," Eric said, his smile spread wider revealing his crooked teeth. "She's gone, Eli. She's gone."

Eli tried to stand. His brother reacted quickly and shoved him back down. He flaunted the knife before Eli's face.

"Didn't you hear me? She's gone, Eli!" his brother yelled. "All gone!"

Eric's laughter echoed through the trees, ringing incessantly in Eli's ears. Stumbling over his hands and feet, Eli struggled to get away. His arms and legs moved slow, they felt heavy.

Then his brother lunged forward, his mouth foaming. As he leaped, his features changed. His eyes rolled back revealing slit pupils like that of a predator. Sharp fangs snapped in Eli's face. Just then, with Eric's teeth threatening to tear him apart, Eli jumped and woke up.

His heart raced as he tried to catch his breath. He rubbed the sleep from his eyes and turned to the side looking for Cali. But he was alone, just like in his dream. And it was quickly getting darker. Eli wanted to get out of the forest now.

"Cali?" He called.

No answer.

"Cali," he called again louder this time.

Still nothing.

He stood up and searched close by for his girlfriend. She wasn't here. There wasn't any sign that she had even been here.

"Cali! Where are you?" he yelled.

He was panicking now. She had to be here. She had to be. Just then he spied movement behind a tree. A figure stepped out in the open where Eli could see. It wasn't Cali though. It seemed too tall. The figure motioned for him to come near.

"Cali?" Eli said, though he was sure it couldn't be her.

The figure motioned him to come closer. But then, what if it was her? It didn't seem right, but maybe. Maybe this was a game. It didn't make sense.

Nonetheless, Eli slowly moved in that direction. Why wasn't she talking? Was it even her? It couldn't be, could it? Goosebumps prickled along his arm.

Someone was watching him. He glanced over his shoulder. It was too dark to see far.

Eli took a few hesitant steps toward the figure in the trees. Cali stepped forward, the last glimmer of sunlight shining on her face. The dark veil shrouding her features melted away, it was her. Her finger was pressed against her lips. Her green eyes were opened wide.

"Don't say anything," she whispered. "Someone is watching us."

Eli followed Cali's gaze, peering into the trees looking for some sign of movement. There was nothing.

"Why did you leave?" he asked quietly.

"I didn't leave. I've been looking or you," she whispered.

"No, I woke up and you were gone," Eli said.

"Shh, I see them," Cali whispered. "Come on, get over here."

She pulled him behind the tree with her.

Eli stared out into the dark, looking for a sign of movement. Some sign of life. He thought he saw something, but he couldn't be sure that it wasn't just his eyes playing a trick on him.

Cali squeezed his hand tight.

"We need to get to the car," she said. "We shouldn't be here."

"Who's out here?" Eli asked.

"I don't know, I just get a bad feeling. Something isn't right," she said.

Which way was the car? Eli looked left, then right. The trees all looked the same. He didn't think they were that far from the road, but the forest seemed to hedge them in on every side with no hint as to the way out.

Eli glanced to his left where Cali stood, her eyes were focused on something a little ways off. He followed her gaze, squinting, looking for something, anything. It was too dark.

Then close behind them a twig snapped.

"Run!" Cali yelled, pulling Eli with her.

They raced through the trees. Ducking between the thick growing pines and the dense underbrush, they moved quick. The ground was soft and springy beneath them, the air cool and crisp against their faces. They scampered over rocks and roots, careful of their every step. One slip would be tragic. There was no way to know if they were heading deeper into the woods or back toward the road. They had to keep moving whatever the case.

Their pursuer thrashed through leaves and branches, edging closer with every step.

They couldn't slow down. Eli gasped for breath. His heart pounded, the blood rushing through his veins like a constant drumbeat in his ears.

From behind them came a horrendous scream. The primal call of some ancient hunter hot on the trail of prey. A chill ran down Eli's spine.

"Hurry, Eli!" Cali yelled pulling him faster.

His feet caught on a branch and he stumbled. He felt a cool touch on his back. Finger nails dug into his skin. The cold hands of death closed round his throat.

Eli's knee dashed into the soft dirt. He scurried forward. His hands scattered dirt and leaves as he tried to find a firm hold. His heel dug into the ground, he found his footing once more and lurched forward. Their pursuers hands slashed at his back, Eli picked up his pace.

They sprinted, fast as the forest would allow. Sweat glistened on Eli's brow. The space between trees grew wider. Blue and purple hues from the twilight sky became visible above. They were nearing the edge of the forest.

"Come on Eli! We are almost there!" Cali ducked between two trees and Eli followed. He could see the road now.

The person chasing them was right behind them. Eli didn't dare look back. It was enough just hearing the panting breaths and heavy footfalls.

The light from the moon now lit their path. Cold air filled Eli's lungs. They neared the road. Freedom was right in front of them.

Slipping past a dense thicket of brush, they crested a slight hill. The road was only a short distance away. Without missing a step, they barreled down the hill and through the trees at the edge of the forest. They emerged not far from the car.

"We are almost there," Cali said.

They sprinted along the dirt road.

Maniacal laughter echoed through the trees and then, that inhuman scream accosted their ears once again. Eli's skin crawled at the sound.

Their assailant hadn't come to the road, but was matching them stride for stride just beyond the trees. Glancing toward the forest, Eli thought he spied a man's face glaring back, but it was quickly hidden among the trees again.

The car was just ahead of them. As they drew near, their hunter resorted to a new tactic. At first Eli didn't understand. The man in the trees seemed to disappear. Then, there was the ping of rock against metal. And still, Eli and Cali rushed forward. A rock whizzed past Eli's head. Another skipped between his legs.

Eli stepped to Cali's right, acting as a barrier between her and the forest. He wasn't a moment too soon, as just then, a rock slammed into his shoulder and another caught him in the leg.

He fought through the pain as they came to the car. Cali quickly jumped into the passenger seat. A stone smashed into the door just as she closed it. Another rock hit Eli in the middle of the back and he stumbled in pain. He hurried around the front of the car. Rocks flew past his face. Just as he opened the driver's door, there was a sharp knock on his forehead. A stream of blood poured into his eyes.

He doubled over in pain as he climbed into the car and slammed the door shut. Rocks continued to bombard the vehicle. A stone hit Cali's window and left a crack running the length of the glass.

Eli stuck the key in the ignition and put the car in reverse. Spinning on the dirt road, he whipped the car around and took off.

"What the hell was that?" he said.

"I don't know. Let's just get out of here," Cali said.

Eli wiped blood from his forehead. The road ahead was blurry. His head throbbed. He gritted his teeth and sped down the dirt road, all the while checking his rearview mirror.

The orange glow of old streetlamps was little comfort as they made their way into town. In fact, Eli struggled to understand how anything could seem so ordinary after what they had just been through. There was a disconnect between life in town and the strange encounter the teenagers experienced just a few minutes away.

They pulled into Cali's driveway. Eli shut the car off and focused his attention on the rearview mirror.

"He's not there," Cali said.

Eli's eyes were still glued to the mirror, waiting for the shadow to emerge in the street. But there was no one. Finally, he breathed a sigh of relief and turned to Cali.

Her eyes were half open and her head drooped low. She turned her attention to her house. The porch light reflected in her eyes.

"Are you going to get in trouble?" Eli asked.

"Probably," Cali shrugged.

"I didn't mean. . ." Eli started.

"Don't even worry about it," Cali cut him off. "I just hope your grandma is okay."

Eli leaned back in his seat and ran his hands through his hair. He wondered if there was any news. Eric wouldn't know. The thought of his brother took him back to his dream. Eric. *She's gone, Eli. She's gone.* Eli shuddered. The words stung. In the dream, it seemed like his brother had been referring to Cali. But now he wondered. What if he didn't mean Cali at all, what if he was talking about Grandma?

Eli's heart sank. He wouldn't know anything until he got home and maybe not even then. He couldn't count on Eric to know what was going on.

Cali took his hand.

"It's gonna be alright," she said.

85

Eli turned and saw the porch light shining bright.

"I'll let you know what I find out," he said.

A gentle smile came across Cali's face. She kissed Eli on the cheek and stepped out of the car. Eli opened the driver's door and was ready to walk Cali to the front steps when she appeared beside him.

"Maybe it's best my parents don't see us kissing on the porch," she said.

"Maybe," Eli agreed. "But if you are already in trouble. . ."

Cali's face glowed in the evening light, the porch lamp added just a hint of warmth to her cheeks.

"No, you're right," Eli agreed. "But thank you for today. I needed an escape."

"It was good until the end," Cali said. She shivered.

"We'll find out who that was," he said.

"It's not important. I'm just glad we're home," Cali said. "I should say goodnight though, before I get in any more trouble."

"Right," Eli said. "Goodnight. Get some sleep."

"You too."

Cali hesitated for a moment before leaning forward and kissing Eli one last time. Eli closed his eyes, he felt Cali smile as she slowly pulled away.

"Dream of me," she whispered.

When he opened his eyes, she was already crossing the front lawn and bounding up the steps. Eli watched her step inside, the front porch light flicked off. He was just backing out of the driveway, when he saw the front door open a crack. He paused, was she just watching him leave?

But then, Cali opened the door completely and stepped outside once again.

Eli parked the car, waiting to see what Cali was doing.

She hurried down the steps and trotted back to the car.

"Ya know, I was just thinking, it's been a long day. But, I'm not quite ready for it to end," she said.

Chapter 10

It was a beautiful night. A few clouds passed in front of the moon, but otherwise the sky was clear. The moon was nearly full, and provided plenty of light to see. Frogs croaked down by the river in the still warm air.

Eli parked the car at his grandma's. He threw the keys on the hook as he stepped inside. He looked around, but there was no sign of Eric. That was just as well.

He wandered out to the kitchen and found a piece of paper on the table with something scribbled on it.

-Grandma is okay. It was a seizure. More tests in the morning. I'm staying at the hospital.

Eli pocketed the letter and went back outside. Cali waited by the car.

"Everything okay?" she asked.

"Yea, all good," he said taking her hand as they started off toward the river.

"Was Eric home?" she asked.

"No. He left a note," Eli said. From the corner of his eye, he saw Cali raise her brow. "Grandma had a seizure. I guess there are more tests in the morning. Eric is staying overnight at the hospital."

"Really?'

"That's what the note said," Eli shrugged. "Surprised me too."

"That's good though right?"

"I guess yea. Good that he can put the bottle down long enough to stay with her."

"You don't think he's drinking in the hospital, do you?"

Eli laughed.

"No. I hadn't thought of that. But I guess he could be."

"Let's hope not," Cali said.

They continued on along the hill beside the river. They walked toward the bridge leading out of town before making their way down to the river. Tall blades of grass rose above their knees and were wet with dew. Eli's jeans became damp where the grass touched.

As they moved closer to the river, the air grew fresh and light. A cool breeze touched Eli's face, on it was the crisp scent of water and the sweet earthy aroma of cattails and berry bushes. The grass dwindled and became sparse as they migrated under the bridge. Here, the rocky shore stretched to the edge of the bridge's concrete abutment on the hillside.

Above them loomed the underside of the bridge. Steel trusses and support beams weaved elegantly together. Through it all was a striking industrial beauty that didn't seem out of place. Where the concrete and bridge came together, there was a small platform where a couple teenagers could find peace. A few large rocks, boulders really, each more than a hundred pounds, were stacked one on top of another against the concrete. The makeshift stairs gave easy access to a small hideout.

Eli climbed up the stones and onto the cement platform. He helped Cali pull herself up beside him. It was a mostly quiet night; the only sounds came from the river. Crickets and frogs echoed their songs. The water lapped against the stones. This is what the ocean must be like, Eli thought.

He had never been to the beach. He had never been to a great many places. There were no family trips when he was a child. There was no vacation or time to get away. That was something other people enjoyed. Eli didn't know that life. The closest thing to a vacation he could imagine was the time he spent with Cali. She was his escape. Were it not for her, he would probably be home, miserable. But that was just some people's lot in life. Some people got to travel the world and have fun, while others lived simple lives of melancholy.

Eli knew, there were places and people much worse off than himself. That thought didn't really bring any joy though. Knowing that his own suffering paled in comparison to the wretched lives of others, often in fact, made him feel worse. His own suffering was not enough. His own depression was not enough. At least he had food and a grandmother that loved him. Some people didn't even have that. What a sad state of affairs is it when one's own suffering is not severe enough to warrant acknowledgement.

"What are you going to do after your grandma gets out?" Cali asked, breaking Eli's trance.

He sat in silence for a moment, watching the water glisten in the moonlight. What was he going to do? He hadn't even really asked himself that question yet. He mulled it over for a minute before answering.

"I don't know," he said. "I have to be there for her, but we'll have to wait and see how things are."

"I mean, like with Eric," Cali said.

"I don't know that either. He's impossible sometimes," Eli said.

He picked up a pebble and tossed it into the river.

"He's not bad on purpose," he said. "Just the drinking. It brings out the worst of him. He can't even take care of himself let alone anyone else."

Eli picked up another stone and threw it across the river. It crashed along the rocky shore on the other side.

Eric would never be able to care for another person. He was trapped in his own downward spiral. Eli struggled to think of a happy memory with his brother. There weren't any, not really. What hurt the most, was that Eli loved him still. Despite all the animosity, all the negativity, Eli still loved his brother and wanted the best for him.

He shook his head.

"If my grandma needs any sort of help, I don't trust Eric to help her. It will have to be me," Eli said.

Cali frowned.

"You think it will come to that?" she asked.

"Who knows?" Eli shrugged. "I don't know how bad a seizure is, but it scared me earlier when I saw her. I thought she was going to die."

Cali placed her hand on his leg. Eli smiled.

"At least I can get away with you. It's corny, but you give me the chance to just breath and get away from all of that," he said. He wrapped his arm around her shoulders. She settled in next to him, her head resting against his chest. After a minute, Cali sighed. Eli slid his arm out from behind her and she sat up. Her hand was still on his thigh, but something had changed in her demeanor.

"What's wrong?" Eli asked.

"Nothing," Cali said. "Well, no, I don't want to go there right now."

"Well, now I'm curious. What were you thinking?"

"It's not important right now. I was just thinking about the future."

"There was more than that though," Eli said.

"Like, how do I say this?" Cali started, she sighed and continued. "I love what we have now. And I love that I can give you peace, but what happens when I'm not here? What if I'm not here to be your escape?"

Eli glanced down, his eyes focused on the grey stones below. His heart began beating faster. He felt the blood move to his face.

"Eli, I love you. I don't ever see that changing," Cali said while taking his hand. "I just don't want to stay here forever. I want to see the world. I want to experience all that there is out there. I want to go to college and learn the history of different places. And then we will go and experience everything together."

"But you are going to leave first," Eli said quietly.

"If I go to college, yea. But I haven't decided yet," she said.

"Why not?"

"It's a lot to think about," Cali said. "My parents really want me to go to this school a couple hours away. It's supposed to be really nice, but I don't know what I want yet. Then I think about us and what it would mean if I went away to college, even just a couple hours."

"No, you can't think like that. It's not fair to hold up your life because of me," Eli said.

"That's the thing though, I can't imagine my life without you. But, I know you hate school. You wouldn't want to go to college," Cali said.

"No, but you can't not go just because I don't want to go."

"Right, but if I went to college how would that work for us?"

"I don't know. We'll figure it out."

Cali sighed.

"I guess what I really want to say is, I worry about you," she said.

"You don't need to worry," Eli started. Cali caught his eyes before he could finish and Eli was forced to glance down. Without a word she had touched something true. She squeezed his hand tightly and consoled him.

"I know how hard it is for you living with your grandma and never really knowing your parents. I know you deal with a lot with Eric and his problems. But, I know it is going to get harder after school with work and being adults at that point. None of this is easy and I like being here for you, I like being the person you turn to when things get difficult. You are that same person for me. I just want to know you are okay, especially if I can't be here with you," she said.

Eli lifted his head and met Cali's gaze once more. Her eyes were soft and searching. Then, taking her head in his hands, he closed his eyes and leaned close, his forehead resting gently against hers.

"I'll always have you with me," Eli whispered.

Cali placed her hand on his chest. Then, she guided his hand to her chest. Beneath his palm he felt the light beating of her heart. Cali's hand moved gradually up his neck. She drew him close, her cheek just barely brushing against his. The smooth cool touch of her skin sent a shiver down his spin. A smile pulled at the corner of her mouth as their lips met. She pulled him closer still as they laid down. Cali's heart beat faster beneath his palm. They sank together, the cold stone unrelenting beneath as their bodies pushed ever closer, but never close enough.

Time passed before they eventually climbed down from their loft. Eli wandered out to the river's edge and watched the water roll over the stones. Cali followed and wrapped her arms around his waist. They held each other by the water until they decided to head back home.

They weren't in any sort of a hurry as they meandered along the river bank and back into town. The night was quiet. Gone was the constant drone of traffic along Main Street. There was no roar of a motorcycle tearing off down a side street or the yowling of a pack of hounds barking off in the distance. It was like a different world at night, absent the sounds so common during the day.

The teens found their way to Eli's grandma's house. They climbed up the steps and went inside. Eli called out, checking to see if Eric had really stayed at the hospital. There was no answer and everything looked exactly the same as when he left.

"I think we're alone," he said.

"You've never shown me your room," Cali said.

Eli smiled. It was true, they never hung out at his house. The place was not the most comfortable. And that was without mentioning the possibility of Eric bumming around. Plus, small and cramped as the place was, it never felt like they could get any privacy.

"It's not much to look at," Eli said. "But I'll give you the grand tour."

He took her hand and led her upstairs, down the narrow hallway to his room. He flicked the light on as he opened the door.

"Ta-da!"

The sweet, tangy smell of body spray still hung in the air from this morning. His bed was just as he left it, the cover thrown to one side, the pillow askew. On his dresser, an assortment of odds and ends, a pack of cards, a stack of old CDs, a hat and a pack of gum.

Cali stepped into the room. She smiled as her eyes took in the new environs. She spied the hat on the dresser and inspected it before donning it herself. She threw it on backwards, her hair flowing neatly out from underneath.

"I think it looks better on you."

"Well, let's not get too carried away," Cali turned to a mirror hanging on the wall opposite Eli's dresser. She tilted her head and adjusted the hat. Smiling, she turned back to Eli who had taken a seat on the edge of his bed.

"I do like it," she said.

Eli laughed.

Cali walked back to the dresser and thumbed through the stack of CDs.

"Do you listen to these?" she asked.

"Here and there," Eli replied. He stood up and strode across the room to stand by Cali.

"This one's really good," he said picking an old case from the pile. He handed it to Cali. She turned it over in her hands and read through the track listing on the back.

"I don't think I've heard any of these songs," she said setting it back on the dresser.

"It's old," Eli said. "I don't even think my grandma was alive when it came out. It's good though, you should listen to it."

"Put it on, I don't have anywhere to be," she said.

Eli popped open the CD case and walked across the room to a stereo placed on the floor beneath his mirror. He dropped the CD in and hit play. A bluesy guitar and a slow piano filled the air.

As he stood up, he looked in the mirror. There in the reflection, he saw Cali gazing at him. Their eyes met in the mirror, for a brief moment something passed between them. It was like she was standing right in front of him, or at least, her reflection wasn't her reflection at all, but really her. The feeling passed as Cali stepped toward him. Her reflection shifted, and then her arms were around him. Mellow guitar echoed off the walls as they tumbled into bed.

When Eli opened his eyes, the room was dark and quiet. The CD had finished playing and the stereo was blinking, waiting to be restarted. Cali was nestled close to him, her head resting on his arm her hand on his chest. His hat was lost somewhere beneath the covers. He brushed Cali's hair out from in front of her face and watched as she slept peacefully.

Why couldn't everyday be like this?

He thought of the gas station. Was it yesterday he applied there? Maybe it was the day before, he thought. He probably wouldn't hear anything back anyway. He didn't have any job experience. The lady at the counter hadn't been very encouraging. But what if he did get the job?

Then what?

He would lose this time. Every day wouldn't be like this. There would be a schedule. His time would grow short, quick. Would he still have evenings like this? Money would be nice, but if it meant losing this, was it worth it?

He couldn't give this up. Wouldn't it be better just to enjoy this summer? Why worry about money? He had one more year of school. Just coast. Coast through this year, enjoy summer. Enjoy the warmth. There'll be enough to worry about later on, he thought.

If they called him back, he would say that he changed his mind. He can't actually work right now. There's too much going on with school or something along those lines, he would think of something clever. Hell, he could just not answer the phone. Problem solved.

This is all he wanted anyway. He wanted to soak up as much of this summer with Cali as he could. Everyday should be like this. It would be.

He placed his hand on Cali's and fell back asleep.

Chapter 11

The first signs of morning were starting to come alive when Eli opened his eyes again. He stretched, an exaggerated sigh emanated from his chest. He reached across the bed, his arms spread wide to open the muscles in his chest and back. As he relaxed, he felt the empty space beside him.

He was alone.

"Cali?"

He rolled over.

The room was still. Eli wiped the hazy fog of sleep from his eyes and blinked. The room remained the same. He listened for any noise. But all was silent. Somewhere out back he heard a pair of mourning doves cooing but nothing else.

He threw the covers back and found his clothes in a pile beside the bed. He slid into his jeans and pulled a fresh shirt from his dresser.

Cali must be downstairs he decided, as he put on deodorant and spritzed himself with body spray.

Where else would she have gone?

He wandered to the bathroom. Turning the water on, he cleaned his teeth before splashing cold water on his face to shake the lingering sleep from his eyes. He ran his hand through his hair, to clear any bedhead. He glanced in the mirror as he dried his face. Water blurred his vision and made his reflection fuzzy, but he thought he looked halfway presentable.

"Cali?" he called again as he made his way from the bathroom and downstairs. Still nothing.

He paced through the downstairs rooms. Cali was nowhere in sight. She wouldn't have left without telling him, would she? Eli glanced at the clock on the kitchen wall, it was only 6:30. Did she wander home in the middle of the night? But no, Eli thought, she was asleep on his left side. He remembered that specifically from when he woke in the middle of the night. He would have known if she climbed out of bed, because his bed was pushed up against the wall and she would have had to climb over him.

No, it didn't make sense if she left during the night. And yet, Cali wasn't here.

Something was wrong.

Eli stepped into his sneakers and went outside. He glanced down the street. It was a beautiful summer morning. The sun was already casting golden rays over the horizon. The sky was mostly clear. The heat from the sun breathed life into the early morning.

Why didn't she wake him?

He wondered as he walked along the street. He would have walked her home at the very least. He couldn't understand why she would just leave. He would ask her once he made sure she was alright.

As he walked he listened to the clop of his sneakers against the damp pavement. It was early, but it was unusually quiet, Eli thought. He glanced at the houses as he walked past. All dark, no signs of life.

When he reached Main Street, he was surprised to find it devoid of the usual traffic. Even if it was still early, you could always count on some vehicles passing through, a semi or a box truck heading to the gas station, a car heading out for an early workday. Somebody was always going somewhere. And yet, there wasn't a car on the road today.

He stepped out into the road and looked left, then right. Not a single car in either direction. Eli clapped his hands in front of him. The sound echoed off the nearby houses and dissipated into the ether. He shoved his fists in his pockets again.

What was going on?

He walked across the road and down the sidewalk to Cali's house. Like the other homes he passed on his street, all the lights were off. Neither of her parents' vehicles were in the driveway. Well, at least there's that, Eli thought. He wouldn't have to wait. He could just knock on the door and see if Cali was home right now.

He trotted up the steps and knocked on the door. Then he waited. Nothing. He knocked again. And still nothing. Frustrated, Eli knocked on the door one last time. The door creaked open as soon as his knuckles rapped on the wood. He stepped back, waiting for something. But when nothing happened, he opened the door and stepped inside.

The living room was dark. Eli flipped the switch on the wall. The overhead light flickered on. Then, with a pop and a flash the light fizzled back out.

"Seriously?" Eli muttered. He walked across the living room to the base of the stairs.

"Cali?" he called.

The house was dead silent.

Eli shivered. None of this felt right. Nonetheless, he felt it necessary to check upstairs. It seemed obvious that no one as home. But if he didn't check upstairs the "what ifs" would eat at him like the dull ache from a sore tooth.

So, he climbed upstairs. He opened Cai's bedroom door first. Her room was neat and organized, the pillows arranged nicely on the bed, but Cali wasn't there.

Eli closed the door and went across the hall to the guest room. That room was less decorated and actually a bit plainer than he remembered. It was empty too.

Last he went to Cali's parents' room. She's not in there, Eli thought. She's not home. But what if? His hand rested on the handle, but he hesitated. No, I shouldn't look in here, he said to himself. What would her parents think, if they caught him here? But really, what did it matter at this point? He was already in the house without Cali's parents' permission, what would a peak hurt?

He turned the handle and opened the door slightly. It was dark. He quickly opened the door all the way, expecting something, but like the other rooms there wasn't anything to see. It too was empty.

Frustrated, Eli closed the door and was about to go back downstairs when there came a loud thud from somewhere below.

He froze.

Someone was here.

His stomach dropped.

Should he hide or try to sneak out? He couldn't sneak out, he thought. There was no way out from up here. He had to hide. Hide and hope. Maybe he could wait and whoever was here would leave, then he could sneak out.

Eli quietly opened Cali's bedroom door and stepped inside. He carefully closed the door behind him. There was a subtle snap as he released the handle. He didn't dare move lest he make any noise. He stayed put, his hands still hovered near the doorknob as he listened.

Everything seemed quiet once again though. He put his ear to the door and strained to hear. But there was nothing. He waited for a few minutes, until it was apparent there was no movement downstairs. He opened the door cautiously and stepped back into the hallway.

Silence.

His heart pounded in his chest. There was nothing to confirm his fears, but still the possibilities rattled in his mind and made his heart race. The blood rushed through his ears. His body was tense.

He started down the stairs, pausing on each step to listen. There was no more noise. At the bottom of the stairs he poked his head round the wall and looked into the living room. It was empty as it had been when he first walked in. He walked through the living room and turned to the dining room and then the kitchen. The downstairs was devoid of any activity. There was no sign of what caused the noise. No signs of life at all.

Eli sighed. Cali wasn't home, that was obvious. But if she hadn't come home, where was she?

Something was wrong. Eli felt out of place. Yet, try as he might, he couldn't come up with a solution for whatever was going on. He would have to sort this out somewhere else though, he couldn't stay in Cali's house if no one else was home.

With one last glance at the living room, he shook his head and opened the front door.

There on the welcome mat was a large rock with a folded piece of paper underneath. Eli knelt and picked up the rock and paper. He looked left and right for signs as to who left the items. Just like the house, there was nothing to see, no one around.

Eli unfolded the letter, still looking out at the street waiting for someone to appear.

The note was addressed to him.

Eli,
Meet me in the forest. You know where.
I'll explain everything there.

There was no signature. Eli's first thought was that it had to be Cali. But why leave a note? Why not just meet him and talk?

He read the note over again and turned the paper over in his hands.

The handwriting was sloppy. The letters scribbled in a hurry with little care. That wasn't how Cali wrote. Her small deliberate print was easy to read and pleasing to look at. This note wasn't from her. But if not her, then who?

Eli put the note in his pocket. He set the stone next to the door and left the porch. With a quick glance down the road, he realized there still wasn't any traffic.

What was going on?

He started off for home, still wrestling with the note and Cali's absence. As he walked, he looked at each and every house, searching for signs of life, activity, something. It was as if he stepped into some long-deserted ghost town. Or maybe he was the ghost. Maybe everything was happening like normal and he was the one who was messed up. But that didn't make sense he thought and quickly brushed the idea from his mind.

Eli picked up his pace, his heart started beating faster once more. He scratched at his palm while he walked, nervously looking from side to side. The hair on his neck rose and an uncomfortable chill coursed down his spine.

Finally, he broke into a run. The sound of his sneakers echoed loudly. His ears were buzzing and his body tense. His muscles all contracted and wound tight like a coil. The air was hot in his lungs as he raced down the street.

He bounded up the steps to his grandma's house and burst through the front door. It was dead inside. Eli slammed the door and sunk into the couch.

His ears were ringing and now the room was starting to spin. Eli closed his eyes and leaned his head back. His stomach turned. Just breath, he tried to calm himself. He slowly counted to ten, then opened his eyes. The ceiling was moving in and out in waves. Eli quickly closed his eyes again.

Rolling to his side and tucking his knees tight to his chest he tried to curl in to a ball and disappear. If only he could make the buzzing in his head stop, he thought. The sound was nauseating.

It was just a spell of vertigo, he tried to convince himself. Nothing more than that. Maybe the heat got to him. Maybe he was getting sick. Whatever the case, it would pass, he kept telling himself.

But the nausea continued. It felt like he was rolling and bobbing, a ship out at sea. But it would be so much worse if he opened his eyes.

Don't, he thought. He curled his fists tight and pressed them hard against his forehead. Don't open your eyes. Don't open your eyes. His body shook.

Frustrated with no relief, he screamed.

The sudden outburst of noise seemed to pop whatever bubble was causing his ears to ring. Still, he felt sick and couldn't stop shaking.

His stomach twisted into a knot. Hot acidic bile rose in his throat. It was all he could do just to roll off the couch. He struggled to his feet and stumbled toward the bathroom, but he stopped short as a sharp pain shot through his stomach. He fell to his knees. Before he could stop it, the contents of his stomach poured from his mouth and onto the floor.

He gasped for breath, the muscles of his abdomen still clenched tight, he didn't know if he would vomit again so he stayed on his hands and knees sucking in air.

After some time, the feeling passed and Eli shambled to his feet. He felt exhausted and disgusting, but the dizziness was gone. He had to clean the floor. But first he just needed sit down for a minute. He plopped down on the couch again and tried not to think about anything. Just be. He breathed slow and deep, letting his mind drift toward nothingness. Darkness and a floating feeling slowly enveloped him. He breathed into it, sinking deeper. His mind was a void, no thoughts, no feelings, just calm. He let the feeling wash over him, cleanse him of all else. Peace and calming filled him. It was going to be okay. He would be okay.

After some time, he got up and cleaned the floor.

He felt dirty all over again. So, he wandered to the bathroom and started the water for a hot shower. He waited until the steam started to fog the mirror over the sink before getting in.

The water alone was a relief. He breathed the steam and let the hot water heal him from the outside in. When the water eventually started to lose heat, Eli turned off the shower and toweled off.

He rifled through his jeans, now laying in a heap on the floor and pulled out the note. He turned the paper over in his hands as he made his way to his room and got dressed.

Eli sat on the edge of his bed brooding over the note. His hair was still dripping wet, a drop fell on the note and cause the ink to smear.

Eli tossed the note on his bedside table. He wouldn't go to the forest, he decided. He wouldn't do that. It's obviously a prank or some weird trap, he thought. The perfect lure from some serial killer. But, no, Eli wouldn't take the bait. He would stay home and maybe call the police, let them know something weird was going on. Let them track down the creep who left this note. They could wander in the woods looking for this weirdo, Eli would wait right here.

But what if?

What if Cali was in trouble? What if she left last night and something happened and now she needed help? What if Eli didn't go and something horrible happened because of it.

He had to go. I should call the cops first though, he thought. He considered it for a minute. No. No, actually, I better not. They would show up and want to know what was going on and all he had was a letter, and a not-so-threatening letter at that. The only thing that made it threatening were the thoughts in his head. Just go, he finally decided.

Eli grabbed the keys to his grandma's car and set off for the forest.

Chapter 12

The woods were quiet when Eli parked the car in the pull-off area. Sweat shined along his forehead. He stepped into the shade of the forest where the heat wasn't as bad. But even still, the sweltering sun was a heavy blanket, smothering everything in its suffocating warmth.

Eli paced back and forth along the edge of the trees. After a minute he stepped back into the sun and leaned against the hood of the car. With his hands in his pockets, he scanned the trees for movement. For some time, there was nothing. Just the trees. Eli shuffled his feet. The silence grated on his nerves.

Then, he saw something. A shadow, just barely noticeable. Something moved behind a tree a little ways inside the forest. Eli squinted. He pulled his hands from his pockets and took a cautious step forward. The shadow moved out from behind the tree. A tall figure, dark, with a hood draped over its head emerged.

"Hey!" Eli called out.

The figure moved slightly. Then, it slowly raised an arm and motioned for Eli to come closer.

Eli shook his head.

"You come out here where I can see you," he yelled.

The figure remained motionless. Then, it turned to walk away. Eli waited. He wanted to call the figure's bluff and force it to come to him. But the shadow didn't turn back, instead it retreated into the woods and Eli was left standing alone.

Eli watched and waited for the shadow to return. Any second now the figure would come back. He was sure of it. He stepped toward the trees, trying to spy where the figure went. The brush was too thick, he couldn't see any movement. He ambled back to the car and ran his hands through his hair. He peered into the forest and then at the car. He wandered round to the driver's side and placed his hand on the handle. He gazed into the dark woods and sighed.

"Fine," he groaned. He walked around the car to the edge of the trees. Then, he took a wary step forward and then another. Eyeing the spot where he had last seen the figure, Eli trudged forward. Not far up ahead the person emerged once again, still dark and difficult to recognize. The figure stood with its hood drawn and arms by its side. Eli moved closer. The figure raised a hand. Eli stopped, he was still about fifteen feet away.

"That's close enough," the figure said, a man's deep voice came from the hood.

"Show your face," Eli said.

Disregarding Eli's demand, the figure posed a question.

"Why did you come here?"

"I don't know, cause I found the note and it said to meet here," Eli said. "You left the note, right? Now, tell me, who are you and where is Cali?"

"There is no one named Cali here," the man said.

"Don't be stupid," Eli said. "Why else would I talk to you? You left a note for me at her house. You know where she's at."

"Follow me," the man said as he turned and headed into the forest.

"No. Not till you tell me where Cali is," Eli said.

The man continued on and motioned for Eli to follow. But Eli remained where he was. His feet firmly planted in the pine needle forest floor. He wasn't just going to follow some stranger into the woods. It was stupid. That's how people died. But then his thoughts ventured to a myriad of terrible situations. What if Cali was being held captive? What if that man saw her walking home last night and kidnapped her? What would happen if Eli just walked away now? He wouldn't know if Cali was trapped and needed help. And what if he was wrong? The consequences would be dire either way. It was a risk he would have to take, he concluded.

Eli sighed and trotted through the trees until he was a few feet behind the man. Then he slowed and matched the man's pace as they trekked deeper into the forest. The man took long strides, moving briskly. His long, dark cloak flicked about his heels as he stepped over roots and branches. As they passed between trees, Eli estimated the man's height. He was a full head and shoulders taller than Eli. He ducked beneath limbs that Eli easily passed under. Whoever he was, Eli was sure he had never met him, he had never seen anyone this tall before.

They weaved through the brush, deeper and deeper into the forest. They were well beyond the point where Eli and Cali had spent the afternoon. As they made their way through the forest, an orange light appeared up ahead. Starting as a pinprick of light, no more than the dim glow of a candle some distance away, the spark seemed to flicker. And as they continued onward, the light grew.

"What's that?" Eli asked.

"You'll see," the man said.

Frustrated, Eli kicked a stick.

"Why don't you just answer me?"

"It's better if you see it," the man said.

"See what?"

The man laughed, but continued walking.

Eli marched along, keeping close behind the man and all the while watching the small round flame beyond the trees. Whether a trick of his eyes or some kind of illusion, the light seemed to grow continually bigger, yet Eli didn't feel they were any closer. A quick glance at his feet quickly assured Eli that he was in fact moving. But how much further until they reached the glowing sphere, one could only guess. It felt like they had been walking for hours and the light was certainly growing larger, but it still felt so far away.

The forest thinned. The trees gave way to open space, dense shrubbery disappeared entirely. The pine needled floor transformed to a smooth dirt surface. The interspersed trees became statuesque watchers, creaking and groaning for a closer look as Eli and the man walked past.

They weaved between the observing trees and emerged on the edge of a hillside overlooking the valley below. To Eli's left the orange light was now completely visible. The light appeared orblike, floating a few feet off the ground. Easily half Eli's height, the glowing mass was actually a cluster of smaller lights all concentrated in the center of a cloud.

Impossible to notice before, the lights were various shades of red, blue, and orange. All similar in appearance, cloudy and translucent, but somehow expressing a defined roundish shape. The colors seemed brightest in the center and became dim toward the edge of the sphere.

Eli took a hesitant step toward the light, curious but cautious.

"What is it?" he asked.

"These are memories, Eli," the man answered. "The various colors are the dominant emotions at the time each memory was created."

"What do you mean memories?" Eli asked. "How are these lights memories?"

"Why don't you have a look? Go ahead and touch one," the man said.

"I'm not touching that. I don't know what it is," Eli said taking a step away. "Why is it just floating there? It's some kind of trick."

"Is it now? I guess it will forever remain a mystery then. Come on, let's head back."

"Wait, where's Cali? You said you would take me to her," Eli said.

"No, I never said that," the man said. "I told you, Cali isn't here."

"What the hell do you mean? Where is she?" Eli yelled.

"I told you she's not here. Cali is gone," the man said.

"And where exactly is here?" Eli asked. "I don't recognize any of this. I've never seen anything like that."

He pointed toward the mass of lights. The varicolored glow gleamed in his eyes.

"Everything will become a lot clearer if you just do as I asked and touch the memories," the figure said. "It's really not that bad. It will help you understand."

Eli remained where he was, feet firmly planted on the ground.

"I only came here to find Cali," Eli said. "If she's not here, I'm not sticking around."

He turned and was about to head into the woods, when he stopped.

"Who are you?" Eli asked without looking back.

"I am someone just trying to help you find your way back," the man said.

Eli turned and looked at the cloaked figure.

"What do you mean, find my way back?" Eli asked.

The man chuckled.

"Don't make me quote poetry, Eli," he said.

Eli didn't move.

"I don't understand," Eli said simply.

"No, you probably wouldn't. Not yet anyway," the man said.

With that, he disappeared. The orange, blue and red lights flickered and went dark. And then, the ground gave way. The earth collapsed, falling in upon itself like a giant mudslide. Eli fought to find solid ground or grab something to steady himself, but it all happened too quickly. Before he could scramble to safety, he was falling through the tangle of branches and dirt.

The entire side of the hill had collapsed and Eli was spiraling to the valley far below. But as he fell his vision blurred and the valley seemed to stretch further away. The faster he fell the quicker the ground seemed to recede from him until he was in a perpetual freefall.

Wind rushed over him, rustling his hair and gluing his eyes wide open. Air filled his lungs, till it felt like they would burst.

Then, the ground disappeared below, replaced by an all-consuming void so dense nothing more could be seen.

Eli descended into that vast dark nothing, the wind whipping against his face and the sound of his own screams filling his ears.

Chapter 13

It seemed forever, plummeting down, down though eternity with no end. All the while, Eli's heart was pounding against the walls of his chest. Every second was worse than the last.

Then an explosion of light. A multitude of colors bombarded his eyes. Reds and golds, dazzling blues and pinks all in fractured rays burst before him. Colors bright to the point of blinding. Eli squinted, but still the lights seeped through and burned.

Then black, the dark once more.

And next he knew, Eli was assaulted by the light again, this time, the colors taking rough shapes that he couldn't fully comprehend. Then dark, and again a return of light. Back and forth, until Eli blinked and everything became clear.

He was in his room, no longer falling. He felt the bed beneath him and to his left, warm soft breathing as Cali's head rested on his shoulder.

His heart was still racing and his head was numb. The terror of the fall still lurked. There was a humming in his ears and a strange almost tight feeling at the base of his neck, like his muscles were stretched taught and wouldn't relax.

He brushed Cali's hair out of her face and she snuggled closer to him and groaned quietly. Eli smiled and kissed the top of her head. He took a deep breath and let it out. He wanted to relax, but his dream lingered. Visions of the forest and endlessly falling flashed before his eyes. His head was heavy with memory and a groggy oppression consumed him. He was awake, but sleep still had hold of him.

He gently worked his arm out from under Cali and sat up at the edge of the bed. Resting his head in his hands he took deep breaths and tried to forget.

A few moments passed in quiet, before he felt Cali's fingers along his back.

"What's wrong?" she said, her voice soft but heavy with sleep.

Eli turned to look at her and took her hand in both of his. He kissed her fingertips and smiled.

"Nothing, just a dream," he said.

Cali smiled. Then, her smile faded and a look of worry came over her.

"What did you dream?" she asked.

Eli stood, grabbed his shirt from the night stand and pulled it on.

"It doesn't matter," he said leaning over the bed and kissing Cali. She wasn't appeased.

"Was I in it?" she asked.

Eli was walking back across the room to the door and stopped. Glancing back at Cali still nestled under the blankets in his bed, he answered.

"Yes and no, I couldn't find you. But you were there somewhere."

"You couldn't find me?" Cali said, a slight smile returning to her lips.

"It was weird," Eli said. "It was more like you had been kidnapped or something and I was looking for you in the woods."

"So, you found me in the end?"

"No, you weren't there," Eli said. "Come on, it's late."

Cali crawled out of bed and they made their way downstairs and outside. They decided to walk to Cali's instead of driving in hopes that she could sneak back inside easier. The street was quiet, a light mist hung above the grassy lawns as they walked by.

"So, you went to the woods to find me? That's creepy," Cali said.

"Well, I didn't find you, but yea."

"Was it like in the movies? Was there an old cabin out in the middle of nowhere?" she went on.

"No, it was the same spot we went to yesterday," Eli said.

"What do you mean?"

"The spot in the woods, by the pull-off," Eli said.

Cali didn't say anything.

"The weirdo chased us out and was throwing rocks at us?" Eli said.

"I don't remember," Cali said. She turned her attention to the blacktop.

Eli stopped, a look of confusion passed over his face.

"Seriously?" he said. "You don't remember running out of the woods. That dude was pelting rocks off the side of my grandma's car."

Cali looked up and met Eli's eyes. Her soft green gaze sifted through memories as she tried to recall.

"Eli, I don't remember any of that," she said after a moment. "I don't remember."

Eli watched her brow furrow as she searched for a memory. After a minute she shook her head.

"We went for a ride and we were talking about getting a cabin in the woods. Not a horror movie cabin but like an actual nice place where we would be cozy," he said.

Cali shook her head.

"I don't . . . I don't remember any of it."

She lifted her head, tears were streaming down her cheeks.

"Eli, I don't remember."

Eli stepped forward and took her hands in his and kissed her on the forehead.

"It doesn't matter, don't worry about it. We are right here now, that's all that matters," he said, ignoring the knot in his stomach. How could she just forget everything from last night? It didn't make sense.

They embraced. Cali's tears falling on his chest left a wet mark on his shirt.

After a few moments, Cali wiped her face. They walked the rest of the way to her house. It was quiet out. No traffic. No sound to speak of but the clip clop of their shoes against the sidewalk. Just Cali and Eli, and that was alright.

They snuck around the back of Cali's place and on to the porch. There Cali hugged him. Her body was soft and warm. His hand rested on her back.

"Sorry about crying," Cali said.

"No, there's nothing to be sorry for," Eli said.

"It's just. I don't know," she said.

"Don't worry about it. You should get inside before your parents notice you've been gone," Eli said.

"Yea. I know," she said.

Before parting, they kissed.

"I do love you, Eli," Cali said.

"I love you too," Eli replied.

With that he left and Cali quietly went inside.

118

He wasn't even down the road when he heard Cali behind him.

"Eli," he stopped and turned.

Cali was on the front porch waving. So much for quiet, he thought. Eli waved back. But Cali motioned for him to come back.

"Something's wrong," she said when Eli reached the steps.

"What do you mean?"

"Nobody's home."

"What time is it?"

The sun was already out and it was comfortably warm, but the morning haze had yet to clear from the air. It was still early.

"I don't know," Cali said. "You don't think they left and are looking for me, do you?"

"I don't know," Eli said. "I hope not."

"I know right? What should I do though?"

"Just play it off. You've been home the whole time," Eli said.

"I was thinking of calling them," she said.

"I don't know. Guess that's up to you. I'd just play it off."

"I guess," she said.

"You gonna be alright?" Eli asked, noticing the worry on Cali's face.

"Yea, it's just weird. I wish you didn't have to go," she said.

"I mean, if they are gone though. . ."

Cali smiled.

"Let's wait an hour and see what goes on. I can't imagine they'd be gone too long, unless they already left for work," Cali said.

"Okay, I'll come back in an hour."

"Good."

Chapter 14

Eli returned home, lonely and confused, but hopeful that Cali would avoid trouble and they could hang out again soon. However, he was unsettled by her behavior. Something was wrong, he thought. How could she not remember anything from the night before? The hair on his neck bristled at the memory of that laughter in the trees. They saw something disturbing last night. Eli couldn't understand how she could forget it so easily. It didn't make sense.

Overthinking the situation would make it worse. He decided not to dwell on it, as best he could. Better to just let it go. Maybe she would remember later. It didn't matter.

As he climbed the front porch steps something made him stop before going inside. A thought, a feeling, something he couldn't quite place, told him not to go inside. But as suddenly as the feeling occurred it passed and Eli continued inside. As soon as the door closed behind him, he knew something was wrong. The living room was dark and quiet, no sign of Eric or his grandma. Up ahead the kitchen was dark as well. A chill breeze passed over Eli's shoulders. He shivered. Hesitating, he called out.

"Grandma?"

Silence.

"Eric?"

Still no answer.

Eli took a slow step forward into the living room. There was a noise in the kitchen. A creaking floorboard or a cabinet door. He froze.

"Hey!" he yelled.

Then suddenly a shadowy figure emerged in the doorway. The figure's face was hidden beneath a black cloak, its limbs buried in the folds of its sleeves. Looming tall and dark, the figure hovered in the doorway before taking a step into the living room.

Eli stepped back. A quick glance of his surroundings showed little in the way of protection. Thinking quick, he reached into the corner behind the open front door. He grasped a short wooden cane, which his grandmother used from time to time.

Taking it in both hands, Eli raised it like a baseball bat and stood his ground.

"Don't move," he said. Though he tried to speak firmly, his voice quivered.

"I'm not here to hurt you, Eli," a man's voice emanated from the figure's shroud.

"I don't care why you're here. You need to leave."

"I will once I have said what you need to hear."

Though the sound of his racing heart pounded in his ears, familiarity assuaged his fear. This conversation already happened. Eli was reminded of his dream and the man in the woods. This was the same man. Only, it couldn't be. That was a dream. The disquieting feeling of déjà vu washed over Eli.

"Get out," he said as he took a step forward. He exhaled slowly and focused on the figure before him.

"Put the cane down and listen, Eli," the man said.

Eli took another step forward and raised the cane even with his shoulders.

"Eli, I already told you she's gone. You need to listen to me. Cali is gone."

Eli froze.

His heart beat furiously, but something inside him had changed. Much as he wanted the man gone, there was another voice in his head that wanted to listen.

"I don't know what you are talking about," Eli said. As the words left his mouth, he felt himself transported out of his body, and it felt like he was watching the scene unfold. He heard his voice, and knew he was the one talking, but it felt like someone else was speaking for him and he was only watching.

"Eli, you do know, you remember your dream. You wish you didn't. You wish it was something you could bury and forget about, but you can't. Deep down, you know I only told you the truth. Cali is gone."

The man's words fell flat. Eli felt like he was floating, swimming above himself and not really a part of this interaction. He watched as he stepped forward and swung the cane at the man. To his surprise nothing happened. The cane slashed through the air. It should have struck the man's ribs. But in an instant, he vanished, melting away into nothing and the cane came down harmlessly.

With a heavy lurch, Eli was thrust back into his body. He stumbled forward and dropped his weapon. He spun around. The room was empty behind him. He looked back where the man had been standing, there was no sign of him.

For a moment he didn't know what to think. Tears formed at the corners of his eyes as a chill ran through him. What just happened? He waited, his feet frozen to the floor. After some time, he collapsed on the couch and breathed a heavy sigh. Then running his hands over his face, he tried to compose himself. But questions raced through his mind.

Who was that?

Eli recognized the man as the same person from his dream. But who?

What did he mean by, "Cali was gone?"

Obviously, that was wrong. Eli had just talked to Cali. She was home, maybe in trouble with her parents, maybe not, but home and fine nonetheless.

And more troubling still, how did he just disappear like that? What really happened there? What had he seen, Eli wondered. It was as though all of it was in his head. A dream maybe. No, not a dream. I'm awake, Eli thought. Something imagined, an illusion. But why?

Stress?

Over what? It's summer, he and Cali were spending every day together. What was there to stress over? The future?

A future where Cali is gone to college and he was left behind. *Cali is gone.* Those were the man's words. Maybe that's what he meant. Cali was gone, or will be, and what would that mean for me? Eli thought. A long-distance relationship wasn't that crazy. It was different, different from seeing each other every day, sure, but it would work out. They would find a way to make it work.

But what if it didn't work out?

It would, Eli thought adamantly.

But what if?

He didn't want to think what that would mean. Cali was his only escape right now. Without her, he would be stuck here. Here with his grandmother and

Eric. He couldn't live like that. He needed an escape. He wasn't going to stay here. He wasn't going to become like his brother wallowing in self-pity.

Cali showed him that there was something better. Something worth living for. What would he be like had he never met her?

He knew his own tendencies. He was quick to choose solitude. It would only be worse without Cali. She made him smile and laugh. She made his heart race. She brought excitement to his life. She was more than just an escape, she was his reason to wake up every day. She was the reason he had anything to look forward to. Without her, he would be lost.

Was that bad?

That his greatest happiness, sometimes his only happiness, came from their relationship? Was that obsession?

Maybe that's where his stress came from. That idea that there would be a time not too long from now, when he wouldn't be able to turn to Cali for an escape from reality. He would have to figure everything out for himself. Like what did he want to do for a living? Where did he want to live? He couldn't just run away from big questions like that forever. He wanted to. He didn't want to think about the real stuff, bills, jobs, the monotonous stuff that consumed the day-to-day. He couldn't imagine what that life was like. He didn't want to know. That was what killed people. That sort of deep-seated unhappiness that couldn't be cured with an escape. It was always there, looming over one's shoulder, watching and waiting like a patient spider. You were drawn into the web and there was no amount of struggle to ensure your escape. Travel too far down that road and there was no turning back. You needed to know the answers before you were asked the questions, otherwise you would end up like everyone else. Running endlessly, searching for something that can't be found. There was no escape. There was no Cali.

Even if he and Cali stuck it out through college and came out on the other side, together, he would have to face all those adult things. It wouldn't always be summer vacation. There would be times, and lots of them, when he would have to face reality. He would need a job, something that enabled him to pay the bills and hopefully something that he would enjoy. It seemed far off, but he knew time passed quickly. At least, that's what everyone said. He would have to figure all of that out. It was a lot. But everyone eventually had to do it. It was just, it wasn't what Eli wanted. He wanted to get lost with Cali and never have to deal with any of the adult stuff.

He sighed.

No hope for the future. No ambition. Just an awesome girlfriend with whom I enjoy being with. Why all the other stuff? Why deal with bills and money and jobs? It all sucked. Yet, that was what you had to do, right? If you didn't, you became like Eric, bumming around your grandma's house with no direction. Eli didn't like either option. He didn't want to be like his brother, that was for sure. But he didn't want to spend his life worried about all the little things either. Why couldn't it just be summer vacation forever?

Chapter 15

The time seemed to slip by as Eli sat on the couch, such that when he decided to go back to Cali's more than just an hour had passed. It was evening when he stepped outside. The sun dipped low toward the horizon, its orange glow colored his face. Where did the day go?

He wandered down the quiet street and contemplated the setting sun.

Cali was waiting on the porch steps when he got to her house. She smiled and hugged him.

"You wanna see something cool?" she said taking his hand.

She led him around the back of the house. At the far back of the yard was the riverbank, stretching from one end of town to the other. Cali quickened her pace as they cut through the soft grass and up the hill. Then just when they neared the top, she told Eli to close his eyes.

Eli did as she asked. Just then he caught a noise, not too far off, it sounded like screams at first, but then he thought he recognized the high-pitched laughter of children.

"What's that noise?" he asked.

"Shh, you'll see," Cali said.

She led him over the top of the dike and carefully down the other side. Eli walked slow, trying not to slip and fall on the wet grass. When they reached the bottom, Cali told him to open his eyes.

A dazzling array of colors bombarded Eli. Reds and yellows, blues and purples, all shinning bright from out on the water. He blinked and tried to clear his eyes.

Overwhelmed and confused, it took him a second to make sense of what he was seeing. It was a carnival. There were lights, games, whirling rides, and tents, all floating on top of the river.

The laughter of children was infectious, Eli couldn't help but smile. The aroma of popcorn and cotton candy wafted on the breeze.

"What is this?" Eli asked.

"It's a carnival silly. Come on!" Cali took his hand and they headed for the river.

There was a wooden bridge leading out to the water. The carnival appeared to be floating on a pier. How it was all held together Eli couldn't guess, but as he stepped out onto the boards, the dock seemed sturdy.

Cali led him, eagerly watching his reaction as he took in the spectacle.

"It's incredible isn't it?" she asked.

"It is. I never expected something like this around here," Eli said.

His eyes were busy following all the lights. Stringers of red and blue were draped overhead with a layer of golden yellow lights above, creating a colorful canopy, beautiful and mesmerizing. There were pavilions with games and prizes on either side of the teenagers as they made their way further onto the pier.

As they walked they came to a fountain. Water spouted above their heads, cascading down in a mist. From the fountain's center, a light shined upward creating a rainbow of colors. Blues and pinks dominated the scene, but scattered among the splashing waters were a myriad of other colors.

Eli stopped, frozen by the beauty of the fountain. His face was aglow in the light emanating from the water. Cali took his hands. She smiled as she gazed into his eyes. They kissed as the warm glow of a perfect summer evening enveloped them.

Up ahead was a giant Ferris wheel at the center of the carnival and to Eli's eyes it looked like the main attraction.

"Do you want to ride it?" Cali asked following Eli's gaze. "We can probably see the whole town from the top."

"I bet we can," Eli said. "Let's go."

Weaving their way through the maze of games and tents and people, they worked across the pier to the Ferris wheel. It towered high above them. The top of the wheel cresting some hundred feet in the air, well above the canopy of lights. The topmost carriages disappeared in the evening sky. That was the seat. Cali and Eli wanted to be at the very tip top.

Though there was a multitude of people, Cali and Eli didn't have to wait to get on the ride. It was like the parting of seas. As they neared the Ferris wheel, everyone gradually stepped aside, letting the young couple through.

They stepped up to the gate and a tall thin man who was working the ride let them through and opened the door to their basket. The other seats already seemed full, almost like everyone was waiting for Eli and Cali to come and take their appointed seat.

The ride began without much delay, in fact Cali and Eli had barely taken their seat before the large wheel began to spin. Slowly rising above the carnival, the Ferris wheel carried them above and away from the crowds. The air was thin and crisp as they rose steadily higher. As they crested the ride's zenith, Eli looked out over top the riverbanks and to the town beyond. Streetlamps glowed like tiny fireflies in the distance. The only view of the town similar to this was from atop the hill on the other side of town, but even then, that view wasn't nearly as impressive as this.

The ride continued to spin, sending Cali and Eli downward back toward the carnival. The lights and sounds and smells all came back quickly as they descended beneath the canopy of lights. Quickly, they ascended once more and were brought back down. Then on their third rotation the Ferris wheel stopped at the top. The noise of the carnival below was a distant hum, the lights, a cozy flame beneath. Everything seemed to fade to the background so that it was just the two of them.

Cali inched closer, resting her head on Eli's shoulder.

"It's beautiful up here isn't it?" she said gazing out at the town. "It's like a dream."

Mesmerized by the lights sprawling out into the distance, Eli agreed with Cali before the cold reality of her words sunk in. It was like a dream. All of this, the Ferris wheel, the carnival, the fountain, all of it was like one big dream. He leaned his head against Cali's and closed his eyes trying to rid himself of the thought.

Feeling her hair, soft against his cheek, Eli was reminded of the reality of this moment. This was real, even if everything else felt out of sorts, there was no faking this. Taking a lock of Cali's hair between his fingers he watched the light reflect in her golden-brown highlights as he gently moved his hand. This was real.

But as soon as that thought settled in his mind and he felt himself relax, a new thought, or actually an old thought consumed him. *Cali is gone.* But yet here he was, with physical proof to the contrary. Still, what did his experience earlier mean, especially now, when it seemed the most obvious? Cali was in fact not gone.

"Cali?" he said.

She raised her head, her eyes green with sparkles of gold from the carnival lights reflected within.

She smiled.

They kissed. For that moment, real or otherwise, there was only the two of them. The world around disappeared to nothing. The only thing that was true was the tender movement of their lips.

Just then, the ride shook and they were roused from their intimacy. They were carried back down as the ride lurched forward signaling a new beginning.

Eli smiled and took Cali's hand. He gladly let go of his questions, at least for now.

Chapter 16

Evening turned to night, Cali and Eli returned home. The house was quiet and dark. No one was home. Where are your parents? Eli thought to ask, but Cali seemed unphased by their absence, so he let it drop.

Cali opened the back door and waited for him to follow before closing it behind them.

Cali took Eli's hands and led him upstairs to her bedroom.

"Close your eyes," Cali said.

Eli smiled and did as she asked. She led him to the edge of the bed where he sat down.

"Wait here. Don't open your eyes."

Then her hands slipped away from his. Eli heard the soft patter of her feet as she left the room. He waited. It was completely quiet. Was he supposed to follow her? No, she said wait here, but maybe she was just teasing him. Was he supposed to actually go and find her? He opened his eyes, the room was unchanged, dark and still.

He stood up and tip-toed across the floor and peaked out the door. The hallway was empty. Then he heard the turning of a door handle, the bathroom door opened. Eli ducked back into the bedroom and returned to the bed, closing his eyes once again.

Cali stepped into the room and slowly made her way toward Eli. There was the slightest movement of air as the door closed behind her. Eli caught the sweet almond scent of Cali's hair as she drew near. Then, she came to a stop in front of him. She rested her hands lightly on his shoulders. Eli fought the urge to open his eyes. Cali's hands migrated slowly down Eli's arms to his hands. She squeezed. Eli felt the warmth of her face next to his, then the smooth touch of her cheek. Her lips brushed his.

"Open your eyes," she said, as she stepped away from him.

There, Cali stood, almost bashful, wearing an emerald dress. Smooth layers of fabric draped over one shoulder, were carefully woven into a flowing skirt that hugged her body down to her waist and streamed loosely along her legs falling just below her knees. She had teased her hair, so that her curls fell to the same side as the dress's shoulder strap, leaving her other shoulder exposed.

Eli's breath caught in his chest. For a moment, he was completely speechless. A shy smile played at the corner of Cali's lips.

"What do you think?" she asked.

Eli rose from the bed and took a step forward.

"I think. . ." he paused and met her eyes. "I think that dress compliments your natural beauty."

Eli met Cali's gaze. The color of her eyes seemed even more vibrant next to this dress, he thought.

"You think it looks good on me?"

"Of course. You are beautiful in everything you wear."

"But it's a dress?"

"What about it?"

Cali sighed.

"It's just. I don't know," she started. "I guess, I just feel self-conscious."

"If you don't like it, don't wear it."

"It's not that. The thing is I really do like it. I love the color and the way it fits me, I feel really good in it," Cali said. Her brow furrowed. "I think maybe part of it is that, I'm not one of those girls that wears dresses."

"I didn't know only certain girls wore dresses," Eli said.

"Well, no. I guess not. But what do you think people will say?"

Eli watched her eyes, looking for truth and answers. Where did this insecurity come from? It wasn't like her. Eli smiled.

"This is what I say, if you like it wear it and don't worry what people say. People always say something."

Cali smiled.

"You said it makes you feel good?" Eli asked.

"Yea it does."

She ran her hand down the side.

"It's smooth. It feels light and fresh, but also, I feel fancy. I don't know it feels nicer than jeans and a tee-shirt," Cali said.

"I think I know what you mean," Eli said. He stepped closer and took her hands in his. "If it makes you feel good, you should wear it. I think you are beautiful no matter what you wear, but that's not important, what's important is how you feel."

Cali leaned close and kissed Eli.

"I love you," she said.

"I love you."

Taking a step back from Eli and letting go of his hands, Cali spun around so that the skirt fluttered about her thighs. Then, she took Eli's hands again and pulled him to her. They fell into a slow rhythmic step. One, two, three. One, two, three. They pivoted and danced slowly across the room. Cali spun, twirling gracefully beneath Eli's outstretched arm. Then as she spun back to him they tumbled onto the bed and Cali fell softly in his arms.

Her hair fell to the side and tickled Eli's cheek, but he barely noticed. He was focused on her eyes, deep dark green with speckles of gold glistening throughout. Cali's eyes were tense and controlled.

The next instant their lips were locked. Eli took Cali in his arms, her body tight against his, never close enough. The single strap of Cali's dress fell from her shoulder. Their hearts beat wildly, passionately, one and one, together. The room faded to nothing. This moment, this feeling was the only thing that mattered, giving and taking, giving and receiving likewise. There were no words, only the two of them, lost in time, but lost together.

Eli opened his eyes, the room seemed bathed in an orange glow. Warm and inviting. He was happier than he could ever remember. He closed his eyes and let the feeling surround him. When he opened his eyes again, the orange was still there, but a cool, greyish purple light now seemed to close in on the periphery. It stole the warmth and took his joy. He closed his eyes again and tried to focus on the orange glow and how it warmed him and made him happy. But the purple refused to leave. The more he tried to focus on the warmth, the more the cold closed in. He fought against it. He didn't want to lose the heat of this perfect moment, but it was no use. The numb grayish purple light was stronger and filled him with empty sadness. There was nothing.

He opened his eyes. All was white, cold and sterile.

"Eli! Eli!"

He breathed deep, cool air filling his lungs.

"Eli! Eli!"

He closed his eyes again.

There was the faintest spark of that warm feeling. Eli didn't focus on it. Instead he took in the moment and let his feelings come and go. Cold and warm, alternated, with the warm light growing hotter with each passing second. The orange light consumed him again, the grey and purple dimmed. He was warm and happy again. He let the feeling course through him and be as it was going to be.

When he opened his eyes, Cali met him. Her green eyes glimmered brightly.

She kissed him.

Chapter 17

"Come on, follow me," Cali said. Eli smiled, hearing the excitement in her voice.

"Keep your eyes closed," she said.

Eli did as she asked, eager to find out where she was leading him.

The grass was soft beneath his feet. The air was warm and full of summer scents, a fresh cut lawn, flowers in bloom, heat radiating overtop of the land giving a slightly burned, but not unwelcome smell. A bead of sweat trickled down Eli's cheek. He wiped it away with his free hand.

"How much further?" he asked.

"We are almost there, just be patient."

They walked slowly down a hill. Eli was cautious, placing one foot tenderly in front of the other. Nearby, the sound of a gently flowing stream came to his ears.

"You can open your eyes," Cali said. She squeezed his hand. Eli opened his eyes and had to blink in the midsummer daylight.

They were down by the river, only it was different. Ahead of them was a large wooden dock stretching down and across the water. Upon the dock was an overwhelming display of bright lights, the sound of music and laughter, large rides including an enormous Ferris wheel loomed in the distance. At first, Eli was overjoyed. Taking in the sights and sounds, he felt like a little kid, awestruck by the wonder of it all. But as the scene sunk in, an uncomfortable feeling that he couldn't quite place settled over him. This was all too familiar, unnaturally so.

"Isn't it cool?" Cali said.

Eli watched her as she took in the lights.

"Yea," he agreed.

He heard his own voice, as though he was talking through a tin can and a wire. He sounded so far away.

Cali excitedly pulled him toward the carnival. Eli hesitantly followed. Cali's exuberance quelled some of his unease. Yet, something lingered inside him, telling him, screaming at him, *"This isn't right!"*

Something was wrong.

"Let's go," Cali said pulling him along after her.

He felt himself torn, part of him wanted nothing more than to follow Cali out onto the dock, but some other part of him wanted to turn and run. He wanted to leave this place entirely. Why did it feel so wrong here? What was going on?

"Cali wait," he said.

She paused, her head tilted a little to the left and her eyes questioning.

"What's wrong?" she asked.

What was wrong?

Nothing.

He breathed deep. The mingled laughter of children amidst the chorus of music and chatter was distracting. Eli closed his eyes and tried to focus. He couldn't make sense why this situation was so unsettling.

"Do you not wanna go?" Cali asked after a moment.

"No, not that," Eli sighed. "I just. . . I don't know, it's weird. I feel like I've been here before," Eli said. No sooner had the words left his lips, when a wave of vertigo came over him. Light-headed and dizzy, he stumbled. Cali held his hand, keeping him upright.

"Déjà vu," she said. "You must have dreamed about the carnival. I've had that before. It feels weird."

"Yea. It's like all of this, I've seen it all."

"You said that already," Cali said, her green eyes searching him. She smiled, "Come on. It's alright. Maybe walking around will shake it."

"Maybe," Eli said.

Together they strode onto the dock and started off through a maze of carnival games. Overwhelmed by the lights, glowing, flashing red and blue and every color in between, Eli's head was on a swivel looking every which way for something out of place. Though he was uncomfortable, there was nothing toward which to direct his attention. For all intents and purposes, it looked like a normal carnival.

As they walked hand in hand through the games Cali's happiness rubbed off on him and Eli couldn't help but smile. The anxiety he had felt, melted away. He found himself enjoying the atmosphere.

That was what Cali always did. She eased his mind. She calmed him and helped him to just have fun. She was his escape, she had always been that to him, and he couldn't thank her enough for the joy she brought to his life.

As they walked through the tents and crowds of laughing passersby they came to a breathtaking display. There in the middle of the carnival the wooden dock came to an end. A large square of wood was cut out and provided an open view of the river below. Only, it wasn't the river they saw. Spewing forth in the middle of that open hole was an enormous fountain, glowing blue and purple and white, the water gushed high above Eli and Cali. A light mist covered a wooden guardrail preventing anyone from falling in. The water splashed and was cool against their skin. Eli turned to Cali. With the dazzling lights behind them, they leaned into one another and kissed. Then, Cali rested her head on his chest. They fell into that comfortable space where only they existed. The rest of the carnival, the games, the sounds, people, it all faded to nothing as they enjoyed each other.

When they opened their eyes again the fountain was still spraying high, but the colors from within seemed brighter. Evening was taking hold. All the carnival lights seemed brighter in the looming twilight. But even more than the sudden increase in artificial light, Eli was struck by something else. Quiet.

With the disappearance of daylight came the disappearance of carnival goers. The laughter and excited voices were gone. Eli glanced left and right and realized they were alone in the dark.

"Cali?" Eli asked. "What's going on?"

Eli turned his attention back to his girlfriend. Her emerald eyes narrowed.

"What do you mean?" she said.

"What do I mean?" he started.

"Cali look around. Where is everyone? Where are the people? They were just here. You saw them," Eli said taking a step back from Cali and waving his arm toward the empty carnival.

"Eli, I don't understand," Cali said. "It was just you and me."

"What are you talking about? They were all right here," Eli said.

"Eli stop it! You're scaring me," Cali said. "It has just been the two of us all day. The carnival doesn't open till tomorrow."

Eli was about to argue, but stopped. His words caught in his throat. This didn't make any sense. He saw the people and he could still hear their laughter ringing in his ears. What was happening? Could he have just imagined all those people? It wasn't like they had talked to anyone. It seemed like a normal happy carnival with all the laughter and chaos that entailed. But what if it wasn't? What if they had never been there, he thought. What if he had just dreamed them up?

"No," he said. "No, you know something is wrong. This isn't right."

"Eli, why are you freaking out, we were having a good time," Cali said.

"Don't you feel it? Tell me I'm not crazy. There were people here, Cali. You had to have seen them. Tell me you saw them," Eli cried. "We can't stay here."

"Eli, no. Come on, it's okay. You just misremembered," Cali said.

"Don't say that. I didn't misremember anything. It was all right here. How do you not remember?"

"Eli calm down, it's okay."

"It's not okay! This is all wrong!"

Eli turned from Cali and as he did, the board beneath his foot cracked. His leg slipped through the dock. Sharp wooden splinters dug into his thigh. He screamed out in pain.

"Cali! Cali help!"

She knelt down beside him. Cali glanced at the dock, where Eli's leg was pinned between broken boards. Blood gushed from a deep wound in his leg. Cali took Eli's hands and steadied her gaze on Eli's eyes.

"Let me try and pull you out," she said.

Between ragged breathes Eli nodded his head.

"Alright. Let's go, let's go," Eli said.

"When I pull, I need you to push up with your other leg okay?"

"I'm ready," Eli said.

"Okay. Now!"

Cali pulled, Eli pushed with his leg that wasn't stuck in the dock. He strained. The wood below buckled.

"Eli, don't let go!" Cali yelled. "I've got you. Come on!"

Eli held fast to Cali's hand. But as he struggled to push himself free, he felt the wood snap. Cali's eyes grew wide.

"Eli!"

There was only a moment between the breaking of the wood and Eli plummeting to the river below. Yet, it passed slowly and he was bombarded with images that didn't seem to make sense. At first, as the wood cracked and he fell through into the crevice he was blinded by the bright lights of the fountain. He turned his head to shield his eyes and everything turned dark. Out of the darkness blue and purple lights mingled and twisted together to form an image. It was strange and obscured, yet Eli recognized a face. His grandmother, but not as he recognized her, her usual soft smile was replaced with a frown. Then, thoughts of his brother came to mind, and he knew why is grandma was sad. He wanted to reach out and take her hand, but even in so doing, the colors changed.

Now orange and yellow warmed him from the inside. The sadness of his grandma was gone, replaced by a new image. Eric, but not as Eli knew him now. No, this was the brother he grew up with. It seemed like a lifetime ago. Eric's hair was long and hung down over his ears. It was six or seven years since Eric had his hair that long. He was laughing, deep, hearty, belly laughs. The way he always used to laugh when the two of them were together. They had been inseparable back then. Eli felt his brother's presence like a warm hug.

The warmth faded and was replaced by cold emptiness. The image of his brother was gone, replaced by an empty room. Eli's heart sank, everything seemed to grow dark once again.

Then an orange light flickered in the distance. The dark was lessened once more and the light grew. Quickly, the orange glow consumed the dark completely and the sadness Eli felt was washed away as he was bathed in the warmth of a summer day. The light continued to grow, larger and brighter than anything he had ever known. It filled him with happiness and warmth. And then just as suddenly as the light appeared everything went dark again. Pitch black and cold, Eli fell into nothingness. Longing for warmth and light once more he cried out. Only, no noise left his throat. Instead cold water filled his mouth. He spat it out and tried to breath, but more water gushed down his throat to his lungs. He was drowning in the dark.

Chapter 18

Something tickled his nose.

"He's doing well," someone said. "Oxygen is at 99."

"Looks like he's waking up."

"He's not fully aware. Give him a little bit."

"Eli, can you hear us?"

A beeping came from somewhere behind his head. Cold air rushed into his nose and irritated his nostrils. He felt like he was going to sneeze.

"You can just nod your head yes or no, okay, Eli. We need to ask some questions and make sure you're doing okay, alright?"

His mouth was dry. His lips were cracked and a sticky saliva film coated the inside of his mouth. He lifted his hand to touch his lips. His arm was heavy.

"Here this will help."

Suddenly a wet towel was dabbed on his mouth. Cool water moistened his lips.

He opened his eyes. Brilliant white light blinded him. His head immediately throbbed. He closed his eyes again, relishing the cool dark. Hesitantly, he opened his eyelids just a crack and peaked at his surroundings. There were people all around him. He couldn't tell how many. Someone patted his lips again with the wet rag.

"I'm okay," he mumbled. His voice was ragged. It took all his energy to say two words. He was so tired. Why did they wake him? Why couldn't they just let him sleep?

"Eli stay awake okay, hun?" someone said.

"I'm okay," he said softly. "Just sleep."

144

"Eli you want to stay awake right now. You can sleep in a little bit. Just try and stay awake, alright?"

Eli opened his eyes. The light burned. But he refused to close them. Something welled up inside him hot and forceful.

"No," he said firmly. "Just leave me alone."

"It's okay, we are here to help."

"No!" he rose up in his bed. Sudden pain shot through his leg. He collapsed back on the pillows.

"Eli calm down, you are going to be okay."

"I don't want to be okay, I just want to sleep," he said through heavy breaths.

He was so tired. Didn't they understand?

Another towel was dabbed on his forehead. He closed his eyes again and leaned back. Pain radiated through his body with every heartbeat. If they would just let him sleep, this would all go away.

"Eli, we are taking some blood okay?"

His eyes shot open. He glanced toward his arm expecting a needle, but there wasn't one to be seen. Instead an IV tube was hooked to the inside of his forearm. He watched a nurse uncap a tube and draw blood from an extension on the IV. His blood dripped into the tube. The nurse capped it and filled another before clipping the extension and setting Eli's arm back on the pillow.

"Can you tell me why you are here?" a nurse asked.

Eli turned his attention to the sound of her voice. She was a tall, red-haired woman. Her eyes were soft and she had a sweet smile that calmed him.

"Where am I?" he said.

"Here," the woman stepped forward and raised a cup of water to Eli's lips. He took the straw in his mouth and drank some. It was cold going down his throat. He took another big gulp and relished the chill.

"That better?" the nurse asked.

"Yea, much," Eli said.

"Alright, tell ya what. I'll give you a few minutes to kinda get your bearings. Then, I'll come back and we can do the questions okay?" she said. "The important thing is that you are awake and okay. If you need anything press this button."

She placed a remote in his hand. With that, she and the other nurses left the room. Once the door closed, the room seemed a lot quieter.

Eli relaxed. As he casually gazed across the room and took in his surroundings his eyes settled on a figure seated in the corner. He hadn't noticed them with the nurses gathered around. The person didn't move. They remained seated with arms folded and head down on their chest.

"Hello?" Eli asked.

The person fidgeted, then lifted their head. The man's hair was shaggy and unkempt and his cheeks were covered in a thick beard. The man turned his attention to Eli. His eyes were soft and sad. Eli recognized him almost immediately.

"Eric?" Eli asked.

His brother stood up and cautiously approached the bed. He wore a dark flannel shirt and blue jeans. He was gaunt. His cheeks were sunken in, were it not for the beard he would look even thinner. As he drew near, Eli noticed dark patches beneath his eyes. He looked rough. Yet as he approached, there was something different about him, a sort of strength that Eli couldn't quite recognize.

Eric crossed the room and sat in a chair next to Eli's bed. He took Eli's hand. His fingers were cold.

"Hey kid," Eric said.

Eli watched him, waiting for something more, but Eric remained quiet. Finally, Eli spoke.

"Where are we?"

Eric chewed the inside of his lip and turned his face away. For a moment, Eli thought his brother might just ignore him. But when Eric turned his gaze back to Eli, there were tears in his eyes.

"I thought I'd be ready to tell you everything," Eric started. "But now that you're awake it's like the words won't come out."

Eric cleared his throat and wiped his face with his sleeve. Then he sighed and looked Eli in the eye.

"I'm glad you're awake," he said. "There was a while there, we thought you weren't gonna make it. You've been asleep for a little over a month."

"What?" Eli said.

"They said you might not remember anything," Eric continued. "It's okay. You're awake now. I'll explain it all. But first, tell me what you remember."

"Remember what?"

"We are in the hospital, Eli," Eric said. "You've been here for five weeks now. You don't remember anything from before you got here?"

Eli tried to think, but there was nothing, only darkness and a feeling of loss.

"No. Tell me," Eli said.

"Eli, there was an accident," Eric said. "You and Cali were involved."

Eric paused and looked away. He bit his lip. Shaking his head, he exhaled slowly and turned his attention back to Eli.

"She didn't make it, Eli," he said. "Cali is gone."

Eli watched the tears form in his brother's eyes. Yet, he didn't register any emotions. He wasn't hurt or upset. If anything, he felt empty, hollow.

"I don't understand," Eli said after a moment.

"It's going to take time, Eli," Eric said.

"No," Eli started. He pulled himself higher in the bed. He fumbled with the remote that controlled the mattress. Eric helped him adjust the bed so he sat up straight. His leg throbbed with every heartbeat. He leaned back against the pillows and rubbed his eyes before continuing.

"That doesn't make sense," Eli said. "What happened?"

"The best they could tell, the police believe the car slid on lose gravel and went over the side of the hill. You broke your leg. Cali died in the crash," Eric said.

"There's this," Eric said as he placed a hat on Eli's lap. Eli took it. Memories came rushing back in bits and pieces, too fast for a clear picture. Cali. Her bedroom. Trees. The smell of sun baked dirt and pine needles. Cali's lips. Then a shadow, on the other side of an overturned Buick.

"She was there," Eli said. "I saw her."

"No, Eli. She didn't make it," Eric said. "Grandma's car was totaled."

"I wasn't in the car," Eli said, the pain in his leg grew worse. "I was outside, she was there, on the other side."

Eric shook his head.

Eli glanced at his brother.

"You weren't there. How would you know what happened?"

"I saw the crash scene," Eric said. "After they brought you here, I went and looked at it myself. There's no way anyone could have gotten out the passenger side. You were lucky, you were thrown out, that probably saved your life."

"I want to see it," Eli said. He pulled the blanket back and started toward the edge of the bed. Pain roared through his leg and up his spine. He froze, the air caught in his lungs. He Leaned his head back and tried to steady his breathing. The pain became worse. It burned deep in his thigh. Eli's body became tense as he waited for the pain to pass. But it didn't subside, if anything it got worse.

"It hurts," said through gritted teeth.

Eric stood up and marched across the room to the door and hollered for a nurse.

Eli sank deeper into the pillows. The pain pushed him toward an all-consuming darkness. He closed his eyes. A few moments passed and then a cool rush of feeling climbed up his arm and nestled in the back of his head. He tasted something almost metallic on the back of his tongue.

"That'll help," he heard someone say, but by the time he opened his eyes he was already drifting back toward unconsciousness. The dark became substance, liquid surrounding him.

Chapter 19

It was cold as Eli felt himself falling, sinking deeper. The pressure building in his chest and pounding in his ears came in heavy waves. *Thump-thump, thump-thump.*

Then, someone emerged beside him. It was too dark to see, but he felt them. It's too late, he thought. The dark has already swallowed me. *Thump-thump, thump-thump.*

There was peace in the dark. Instead of fear and anxiety, Eli almost welcomed whatever was to come, whatever was waiting deeper beneath.

But he wasn't given time to experience that. Suddenly, he was being pulled forcefully upward. The dark subsided, and the heaviness became light.

They broke through the surface, and Eli gasped. Breathing deep, the crisp night air filled his lungs. Someone helped him out of the water and back onto the dock, where he collapsed on his hands and knees. Eli coughed. Water retched from his stomach. He fell to his side. His heart raced as he tried to catch his breath.

Beside him, Cali stood drenched. Her dark hair plastered flat against her head. A puddle of water formed at her feet. She had her hands raised behind her head. Her chest heaved as she breathed deeply. After a minute, she knelt beside Eli and took his hand.

"Are you okay?" she asked.

Eli nodded.

Cali smiled, but the joy faded from her face when she turned her attention to his leg. She touched his thigh. Pain radiated through him. He yelped and jumped back from her touch.

"We need to get you to the hospital," she said.

Eli glanced down at his leg. Dark blood stained his jeans just above the knee. He squeezed Cali's hand. Then he turned his eyes to her and focused on her soft expression.

"Please don't leave me," he said.

"I'm right here," Cali responded.

"Just please, stay here with me," Eli said.

Cali squeezed his hand.

"I'll always be with you."

The dock beneath them shifted. Loose boards creaked. Water splashed against thick support beams below.

Eli tried to lift himself, only to discover his leg was too weak to even stand. Cali supported him. She eased him into a seated position.

"Cali don't leave," Eli mumbled.

He sank into her arms. His leg throbbed. Each heartbeat caused a deep ache in his thigh. He wanted to close his eyes, to sink into nothingness, leave the pain and confusion all behind. But there was no escape. The pain would remain. Cali was his only relief.

Cali is dead.

The words rang in his ears like a bell.

Cali. Is. Dead.

He clutched her hand. Tears welled in his eyes. She wasn't dead. He felt her body warm against him. She squeezed his hand.

Cali was very much alive.

"Cali?" Eli whispered.

"Eli, I'm right here," she said. Her voice grew distant. Eli fought to stay conscious, but he felt himself slipping. His head was heavy, he struggled just to hold himself upright. He was slipping back to the unknown, to a place where nothing could be trusted. Or was already there? How could he know?

Cali held him tight. He could hear her heart beating.

His eyelids drooped. Tears clung to his lashes and blurred his vision. He blinked, but a thin film, like faint smoke from a small fire, seemed to coat his eyes. Sinking deeper into his mind, it clouded his thoughts. It seeped through his being and refused to let go.

"Cali! Cali!" Eli cried.

There was no response.

The fog became darker and denser. It blocked all light and muffled all sound.

"Cali! Don't go! Don't leave me, Cali! Don't go!"

The fog drowned out everything. All turned to grey.

"Eli wake up! Wake up!" someone cried from far way.

Chapter 20

The IV drip squawked for a nurse. A red light near the side of the bed blinked in accordance with the high-pitched beeps. Eli turned his head toward the IV pump and watched the light. The room beyond faded to nonexistence. The light occupied all his attention. Beeping slowly, calling for aide, it was a beacon. A nurse's beacon. They would come running soon.

Not really.

It wasn't their fault. Sirens just became background noise after a while. An incessant beep to a patient was just white noise to the nursing staff.

It was starting to become background noise to Eli now. The light lulled him. If he focused on it long enough he would drift back to sleep. The IV sound would continue on and mingle with his dreams. And sometime later he would wake to discover the beeping was always in his head.

A doorway on the other side of the room opened. Fluorescent light from the hallway flooded the room and caught Eli's attention. He turned to the new stimulus and saw a nurse, answering the beacon's call.

She waltzed over to the machine and clicked the stop button.

"Thirsty, I see. Drank all your fluids already," she said.

"My mouth is dry," Eli said.

"Did you drink your water?"

"I have water?"

The nurse pulled his food tray closer and handed Eli a Styrofoam cup with a straw poking out of the top.

"Thanks," he said.

"How do you feel?" she asked.

"Fine, I guess."

"How's your leg?"

"I don't know. It doesn't hurt right now."

"The morphine seems to be working then. We'll keep you on 15 milliliters for now. Let one of us know if the pain starts to creep back up though, we can go higher," she said adjusting the pump below the IV drip.

Eli watched her adjust the clear rubber tube. She worked deftly, her hands smooth and rhythmic as she placed a new fluid bag on the metal stand. When she finished, she adjusted the blanket on Eli's bed.

"Can I get you anything else?" she asked.

Eli was quiet for moment. He didn't need anything, not really.

"Is she really gone?" he asked.

The nurse pursed her lips. Her eyes searched Eli.

"Yes," she said, stepping away quietly as Eli turned his attention toward a blank section of wall. He did not cry. No tears formed in his eyes. He stared blankly at the wall. Waiting for something. Anything.

Enough with the joke. Where was the punchline? Where was the plot twist? Was the answer simply, yes. Yes, your girlfriend is dead. Yes, she is dead because of you. Yes. Yes!

No. No, it wasn't that simple. It couldn't be. Cali wasn't dead. He saw her.

She was a shadow on a summer's day. A moment forever burned into his mind. She was alive. Eli knew that for certain.

He drifted off on waves of haze. His thoughts guided him back to the day of the crash. The hot sun reflected off the overturned car. Dust swirled. There was movement, a shadow on the opposite side.

This was exactly as he remembered it. This was the truth. No matter what anyone else said. He saw her shadow with his own eyes. He knew the truth.

Eli propped himself up on his elbow. Cali ducked behind the vehicle. Her shadow disappeared from view. Eli watched, waiting for her to emerge from one side or the other. But the dust settled and there was no more movement.

She was still there. He knew it.

Struggling to his feet, Eli stumbled through the underbrush toward the crash scene. The earth moved slowly beneath him and Eli noted the marks of the devastation as he worked his way down the hill. Small bushes were crushed, rocks scattered, a deep gouge was carved into the face of the hillside where the car slid on its roof. It was an ugly scene, Eli thought.

He neared the vehicle. The earth shifted beneath his feet. Loose dirt slid down the side of the hill. Eli stumbled to the wreckage. He leaned on a smooth section of the car as he carefully made his way to the other side. It creaked and shifted slightly beneath his touch. The passenger door was open, Cali lay just a few feet from the vehicle.

She was sprawled on her backside. Her eyes were closed. A layer of dust had settled over her. Eli knelt beside her and lightly touched her shoulder.

"Cali? Can you hear me?" he asked.

She stirred beneath his touch.

"Eli," she gasped as her eyes shot open. "Eli what happened?"

"Shh shhh. Don't worry. What hurts?" he asked. He gently brushed her hair out of her face. Dirt was caked to her forehead and cheeks. Cali moved her left arm and revealed a dark stain on her side. Eli froze.

"Eli, it hurts," she said as she tried to lift herself. Her hand went to her side.

"Cali don't. Just stay where you are. Let me look at it," Eli said.

He moved to Cali's left side and turned her slightly so he could see the wound.

"I'm going to look okay?" he asked.

She nodded.

Eli lifted the corner of Cali's shirt to just below her ribs. There, along her side about level with her navel, was a deep gash. The skin was split wide, a piece of class wedged deep in the wound. Blood seeped from the lesion and down her side. Eli touched the tips of his fingers below the cut. Cali shuddered.

"Shoot," he muttered.

"It's bad?" Cali asked.

Eli couldn't hide the truth. He met Cali's eyes and nodded silently.

"Eli, help me. What do we do?" she asked.

"We need to get help. I'm afraid to move you though. There's a lot of blood," he said.

Cali's eyes grew wide.

"Eli don't leave me," she said. Her voice cracked. "Eli please, don't leave."

Eli glanced over his shoulder and back up the hill.

"We need help."

He ran his hand through his hair. He had to do something. But what? He couldn't leave her. He wasn't sure how much blood she had lost or how deep that piece of glass was lodged in her side. He didn't dare remove it for fear of making it worse.

Easing her over gently, Eli helped Cali roll onto her back once more. But in doing so she seemed even more uncomfortable. Her breaths were sharp and shallow.

"Cali look at me," Eli said.

Her eyes found his. Her glassy stare intense with fear. She gasped for air.

"Eli, I don't want to die."

"Cali, no. Don't think about that. We are going to get you help."

She clawed at his hand. Then, struggling to breath she began coughing. Her face twisted in agony as each cough put pressure on her wound. Blood dripped from the corner of her mouth.

Eli lifted her head and wiped the blood away.

He glanced back up the hill. It was a steep climb. They couldn't stay here though. No one would see the car from the road. No one would come to help them down here. They had to get back to the road. It was their only hope. Cali would die otherwise.

Eli turned his gaze to Cali. He breathed deep.

"I need to carry you. We can't stay here," he said.

Her eyes were distant. She nodded slowly.

Eli placed one arm beneath her shoulders and lifted her to a sitting position. Then, he carefully lifted her lower half with his other arm and stood. She wasn't heavy, but it was a long climb back to the road.

A thrum of electricity ran through his body as he set off. His feet dug into the loose dirt. The muscles in his legs contracted and propelled him upward. He held Cali close. Her body was slight in his arms and her hand gripped his shirt tightly.

Eli worked his way up the hill, stepping carefully over stones and branches. Each stride was focused and intentional. He was well aware of Cali's pain. The last thing he wanted was to add to her misery. He had already caused enough trouble.

They climbed quickly. Eli's heart pounded loudly in his ears. They crested the embankment and Eli stumbled out into the road. His knees shook as he crouched down. Cali slid from his arms.

Her face was pale. Her eyes were vacant as she gazed up at him.

Now what?

They were on the road, but they were still alone.

Eli stood. The setting sun cast an orange glow over the valley. Warm and inviting, the feeling was at odds with Eli's racing thoughts. He needed help. He couldn't carry Cali all the way back to town. She would die before then. Time was slipping away. The sun dipped further beyond the horizon. The last golden rays of daylight mingled with the blue and purple lights of evening.

"Eli," Cali whispered.

He knelt beside her once more. She was fading fast. The light vanished from her eyes, vivid green turned to grey. Her lips were pale. Eli took her hand; her cold skin sent a shiver up his spine.

"Cali, stay with me. We are going to get help," Eli said.

He kissed her forehead.

"It's going to be okay," he said.

158

A slight smile crossed Cali's face as she tried to focus on him.

"I love you, Eli," she said softly.

"I love you too."

There was a glimmer in Cali's eyes, a small spark, like the twinkling of a star. Then, the light extinguished. Her last breath passed through her parted lips. She was gone.

"Cali," Eli said, cradling her in his arms. "Cali! No, no, no."

Eli choked on his words as tears streamed down his face.

"Cali, I'm right here. I'm still here. Don't go."

The setting sun disappeared behind the hillside. A wave of clouds rushed forth. Heavy drops of rain tumbled from dark skies. The teens were drenched in the cold, clinging rain. Holding tight to Cali's lifeless body, Eli buried his head in her shoulder.

Cali was too young. She was going into her senior year, she would turn seventeen this summer. This wasn't when she was supposed to die. She had a whole life yet to live. There were still joys and pains she was supposed to experience.

They weren't supposed to be separated like this, before life even began. Their story wasn't even half told. How could it be over?

Eli wept.

If it was a children's story, Eli's tears would have mixed with the rain and saved Cali. Through some unknown magic, his tears would have brought her back to life. There would be joy. The sun would return and banish the dark clouds of misery. Not even the power of death could rein in their unbridled love. Happily, ever after.

But it wasn't happiness that Eli felt when Cali's hand moved along his back.

Her fingers found their way to the nape of his neck and passed through his hair. Eli felt her chest rise and fall as she took a deep breath.

Horrified, he raised his head and saw her eyes, vibrant and full of life, gazing back at him.

"Eli," she said. "I'm right here."

Her voice was like a winter wind, freezing Eli to the bone.

"Cali," Eli sighed. "Cali, how?"

"Eli, just relax, ok? Everything is going to be alright."

"No. This is wrong," Eli muttered as he backed away. He slid sideways in the mud, his eyes focused on her reanimated body.

"Cali you were gone."

She raised her hand as if to console him, but Eli brushed her away.

"Eli, you're going to be okay. Don't worry, okay? I've got you," she said.

"Cali, stop. I'm fine. It's you I'm worried about. I saw you die, Cali. I held you in my arms as you stopped breathing. I watched it happen. I watched you die."

"Eli, don't worry. Everything is going to be okay."

Eli moved to stand up and a sharp pain shot through his leg. He glanced down and saw a deep gash running down his thigh. His pantleg was red with blood.

"Eli, just stay where you are. Help is coming," Cali said.

Eli raised his head, Cali kneeled next to him. Her hand was on his shoulder and the lights of the carnival shined bright behind her.

"Just focus on me, Eli. You are going to be okay. You lost a lot of blood."

"No, I'm okay. I'm okay," Eli said. "But, you. You were bleeding. I saw it Cali. I saw you die."

He paused and took in the scene around them, lights above and a river beyond the dock where they sat.

"What is this? How did we get here?"

"Eli focus on me. Look at me," she said brushing the hair from his face. "We are at the carnival, remember? The dock broke and you hurt your leg. I already called for an ambulance. They're gonna be here soon. I know it's hard, just try and stay calm. It's going to be okay."

Eli gazed at Cali. Her brow was furrowed. Her eyes glistened in the carnival lights. Tears clung to her lashes. She bit her lip.

"Cali, I just want to go," Eli said.

"We can leave soon, Eli."

"No. I just want to leave with you. Help me up. Let's leave."

"Eli, we need to go to the hospital for your leg. You need to see a doctor, it looks really bad," Cali said.

From off in the distance there came a sound. Like a ringing bell, the sound started soft, but grew louder and harsher the longer it went on. Eli turned toward the sound. As the ambulance drew nearer the siren's scream was unrelenting.

Eli found Cali's hand and met her eyes.

"Cali please! Just help me up. I can walk once I'm up, just please help me."

"Eli don't. Just stay there, the ambulance is only a couple minutes away."

"I know! I can hear them. That's why we need to leave. I don't want to go, Cali. Please. Please don't make me go," Eli said.

"Eli, you need help. Your leg is really messed up. I'm sorry. You can't even walk right now," she said.

Eli fixed his jaw and pulled his hand from Cali's. Then using his arms for support, he tried to lift himself up.

"Eli, stop! You're going to hurt yourself more," Cali said.

Eli focused on Cali. She rested her hands on his shoulder, but he shrugged her off and tried to fight through the pain. It was no use. His leg couldn't support him. He barely put pressure on it and a wave of pain surged through his thigh. He fell. Cali was there to support him. Frustrated, Eli buried his face in his hands.

"Cali. . ." Eli trailed off. The pain was too much.

"Eli, I'm right here. Don't close your eyes again, stay with me," Cali said.

Eli fell back. The stars above were blurred by his tears as he stared heavenward. What was happening? How did he get here?

Moments later, a team of EMT personnel lifted Eli onto a gurney and wheeled him to the ambulance. As he was rolled into the vehicle, he saw Cali standing nearby. Her hair was messy and her shirt was soaking wet and clung to her shoulders. But in that brief moment, Eli saw something more, a light or perhaps an aura surrounded Cali. Maybe it was just the flashing lights or the glow from the carnival. He couldn't say.

The door closed and the ambulance sped off.

Chapter 21

Great waves swelled and rolled, rising high above the highway. The dark waters rose and fell like the breast of some great beast. The lake grew, consuming swaths of open land. Mighty pines and cypress trees were buried beneath mammoth waves. The great sea climbed higher, looming above the road like great thunderclouds.

Eli slowed the car to a crawl. The lake had been mostly dry for ages. Eli's eyes were wide with disbelief as he watched the waters, thrashing and churning, breathing. The road followed the edge of the lake and rose over a hill near the dam that served as the lake's northmost boundary. The water swelled above the roadway, even the top of the hill. It soared like a great mountain, threatening to wash away the asphalt and bury the works of man beneath the power of nature.

The car slowly ascended the hill. The waves glared down, ready to collapse in one enormous wave. But the wave didn't fall, at least not yet anyway. Eli drove on, up the hill and onto the next. Now high upon the hill that served as the lake's dam, he looked back. The waters were retching to and fro. Waves rising and falling in great swirling masses. Eli stopped and stepped out of the car.

He climbed over the guardrail and waded through knee high grass to a line of boulders overlooking the lake. The large stones sat on the very edge of the hill and provided a perfect view of the valley and lake below. Eli peaked over the top. The lake thrashed before him. Dark clouds dominated the skies above the raging sea. Great waves crashed over the dam. Cold water, splashed across the boulders, drenching Eli.

There was movement to Eli's left. Then, the screech of wet shoes on slick stone. Eli turned, just in time to see Cali clamber up and on top of a nearby rock. Eli broke out in a cold sweat. He started to call to hear, but upon seeing her feet slide on the slippery stone, he held his tongue. Cali skittered across the boulder, perilously close to the edge. She swayed with the tempest winds, her arms held out at her sides to steady her. Eli offered her his hand, but his feet remained firmly planted on the ground.

Cali glanced at him and smiled, but she didn't take his hand. Instead, she continued on across the slick rock. Eli glanced out across the waters and then back to Cali. His heart raced. He breathed deep and started up the boulder. As he climbed atop the stone, the wind whipped his face and the waves seemed to grow larger. The rock was too slippery, too dangerous. But Cali wandered freely, flirting with disaster. One wrong step and she would fall. He needed to get her away from the edge.

"Cali!" he called out.

Water from the waves cascaded like rain and poured down on her. She didn't turn. She didn't acknowledge Eli whatsoever. She continued dancing along the rockface.

Eli's shoes slipped upon the wet stone surface. He breathed deep and tried to steady his nerves.

"Cali, come on!"

Eli inched further out onto the stone. Cali continued her dangerous game. Eli followed her, drifting further toward the edge.

"Cali! Please, come with me," Eli pleaded.

Cali smiled and took one step back toward him.

"Why don't you come with me?" she said as she took his hand.

With a swift turn, she pulled them both over the edge.

Eli screamed as they rolled through the air. The waves crashed around them and they plummeted down into the abyss. Eli's voice was drowned out by the rush of water.

But as they fell, the waves rose up and cradled them. Almost guiding them safely through their decent, the water wasn't harsh and unforgiving. It moved with them, holding them, protecting them. It guided them down below the dam.

"Eli, relax," Cali's voice chimed in his ears.

He turned toward the sound of her voice. But he was alone, drifting through the waves.

"Cali?"

"Just relax, Eli," she said softly, her voice melting into the sound of the water.

Eli breathed deep and exhaled slowly.

The water rushed around him. Waves crashed and swirled as he fell. It seemed an orchestra of violence, waves swelled in crescendo and drifted quietly away in diminuendo. But through the violence, the water never hurt him. Eli fell softly, sinking deeper into the waves, like falling into a soft bed. The water embraced him, holding him close, tighter and tighter until the border between water and man was blurred. Seeping through his pores and streaming in his veins, the water became him. Blood to water, his body dissolved.

There was no pain, no harsh separation of body and soul. If anything, the transfusion was natural. This was the way, the evolution from one phase to the next. A passing on of things lesser to an amorphous body. A body without bounds, limitless, falling and rising endlessly with the waves.

The water was not bound by the confines of land. The lake was a segment, but not the whole. Streams and rivulets diverged from one body, coursing over rocks and around bends, the land was a guide to a greater end. The water flowed beneath a bridge on the edge of a small town. There were stones below and others skimmed across the shimmering surface as two teens spent a summer afternoon skipping rocks.

The water raced down a small hill and merged with a larger river, rushing forth, onward, toward the ultimate destination, the place where all water goes. Speeding through valleys and wide swaths of land, marrying, joining, all became one in the great vast ocean.

Crashing and swelling, the waves breathed with the wind. On the surface, the visible motion of the sea manifested itself with water splashing over a smooth sandy beach or against a stony shore. Strong winds across the surface gave rise to great breakers. Below the surface, the interplay of tides pulled the ocean this way and that, rising and falling with the passing of the day and the phases of the moon.

Great swirling masses of ocean fed the skies above. Dark clouds soaked up the salt water like a sponge. Heavy thunderclouds formed, as impossibly small droplets of water were absorbed. Gorged by the heavens, the water became one again. The clouds grew to colossal proportions, ever darker and ready to burst.

Then, when the time was right, the skies relented.

Wrenched from their makeshift home above, raindrops were cast to the earth below with terrible fury. They sped through the skies to their eventual doom below.

A barren riverbed, thirsting for rain struggled to contain the sudden onslaught. Sunbaked dirt soon turned to mud and then flowing water. Upstream, a fallen tree, smothered with debris chocked off the waterway.

With nowhere to go, the river backed up and spilled over the embankment.

The water marched inch by inch toward a small rural town. Creeping over sidewalks and down cellar walls, the water was a deceptive force of change. Always stretching further and seeping deeper, it uprooted gardens and plants, transforming the landscape with remarkable ease.

The land, which took so much from human hands to tame, was forever altered in one afternoon by an angry storm. And thus, it was, that a small acorn, unnoticed at the bottom of a brush pile, was caste forth from a fiery fate and sent floating. On it went, bobbing along, eventually finding safe harbor upon a slight hill in the middle of a field once the waters started to recede.

The water-softened-earth on the little hillock where the acorn came to rest was the perfect home for the nut. In the weeks following the flood, the acorn took root. A year later, a small sapling emerged atop the little hill. In five years, the tree stood just over ten feet tall and proudly looked out over the field. Ten years later, the tree had tripled in height and width. Its thick gray brown bark was still mostly smooth, but some noticeable vertical fissures had emerged. At thirty years old, the tree was some fifty feet tall. Gazing out over the field, the gnarled gray bark was thick and strong from many long winters. In summer, the dense crown was home to a pair of hawks, who from their lofty perch had a perfect view of the field. In fall, bright red leaves burned like fire.

It was the middle of summer and the leaves were still dark green and full of life. At the base of the tree a young boy played with a fallen limb. He jousted an invisible foe, ducking and side stepping his enemies' attacks. The boy was quick and agile. He sprung forward and then quickly back pedaled toward the safety of the tree. The invisible enemy was putting up a fight today. The boy jumped and vaulted himself off the tree. He landed gracefully on his feet, but still chose to roll through the grass. Then with one last heroic flash of the blade, the boy struck down his last invisible enemy. The battle was won.

The tree sighed. It's leaves shuddering lightly as it watched.

Twigs all in his hair and a smile on his face, the boy laid his sword at the base of the tree. It would stay there until the morrow, when foes were bound to return. A day's work done, the boy wandered off across the field toward home.

He returned the next day. And the day after. Every day that long hot summer, the old oak watched the boy play at swords. Then school came and the fighting lulled. The enemy was none too keen to attack as the days grew shorter. The boy would still defend his claim, but the battles weren't as brutal. The enemy was on the ropes. Come winter, the boy rarely had to defend the tree. So, defeated was the enemy, that the boy and tree slumbered all winter long. But it was in those cold nights that the enemy grew strong once more. Come spring, the boy was required to pick up his sword again. He shook off the rust, a long cold winter had made him clumsy. But his old prowess with the blade still lurked beneath the surface and soon he was fighting as well as he ever had. It was a valiant struggle. The spark of war rekindled. A long summer of invisible bloodshed came and went. As did another fall and winter. Spring and summer returned with the promise of more sword play. For years, the tree watched the boy fought battle after battle. And slowly, like leaves changing from green to red, the boy stopped coming to the tree. The enemy was defeated and there were other battles to be fought and won. Then one day, some few years later, the boy returned. Only he wasn't alone. With him was a girl. They laughed and played as young couples do. There was love between them. They leaned against the old oak and watched the sun settle over the hills. The tree sighed and the air it exhaled was taken in by the boy. The light from the sun faded, but the couple remained. They left late that night, and returned the next day. And the day after that. Similar to those days of war years before. But there were no battles now. It was peacetime. A time for love.

Eli breathed deeply the sweet earthy air beneath the oak tree. Cali rested her head on his chest. Eli listened to the sounds of the night, an owl called from some distance away, there was the rustle of grass as deer meandered through the field, and the soft chirping of crickets and frogs by the river. It was a warm night, a perfect summer night. The cares of the world were far off and all that mattered was this moment, beneath an old oak tree.

As Eli soaked in the moment, he relished the warmth of the night and Cali's body next to his. There was comfort in warmth. It felt right.

By some trick of the moonlight that Eli couldn't understand, there was a warm amber glow that seemed to wrap around the two teens like a warm blanket.

Eli sank into the tree and let the feeling wash over him. He could stay in the warmth of this moment forever. He would hold on endlessly if that's what it took to ensure this peace never ended.

Chapter 22

Eli awoke suddenly, wrenched from peaceful dreams to the horrible reality of life. The air was stale and hot. Fragments of dust floated in a bright bar of sunlight that shined through a window. The beam of light stretched across his bed, suffocating Eli with its stagnant heat.

Eli shifted his hip on his pillow, relieving the pressure in his broken leg. He turned slowly to the bedside table next to him and glanced at an orange bottle. Doctor's notes were strewn across the wooden stand beneath the prescription pills. Eli tried read the papers some days before, but it was hard to focus.

He picked up the bottle only to find it nearly empty. There were just two tiny pills inside.

Closing his eyes, he leaned back into his pillow. The pain would return soon if he didn't take the pills. But the pain would return anyway, what was the difference between an hour or six? The pain would return and with it the crushing weight of life. He could postpone that feeling for a little while, but there wouldn't be any more pain relievers. Not for a while anyway.

Eli licked his lips. His mouth was dry and his breath stank. There was a glass of water on the bedside table. The sunlight was refracted in the water, casting a rainbow of light onto the floor. Tiny particles hovered, suspended in the water.

He drank, nice and slow, letting the water trickle over his tongue and down his throat.

There was a knock on his door.

Eli glanced at the pills then back at the door.

He poured the small white pellets into the palm of his hand and considered them.

There was another knock.

Eli looked up. With a sigh he dropped the pills back in the bottle and returned it to the wooden stand.

"Come in," he croaked.

"How ya doin'?" Eric asked as he entered.

Eli watched his brother casually stride across the room. He looked healthy. His thick brown beard was growing nicely. His eyes were vibrant as he inspected the room. Eric moseyed to the window and toyed with the edge of the curtain.

"Fine," Eli said.

"Fine," Eric said. "You don't sound fine. You sound like a frog."

"I just woke up."

Eric pulled at the curtain. It slid along the aluminum hanger and shut out much of the sunlight.

"How's your leg?" Eric asked.

"Still there," Eli replied.

"They said they could take the cast off in another three or four weeks," Eric said.

"That quick?"

Eric smiled weakly.

"I know it's a long time," he said.

"You don't know."

"Maybe not," Eric said. "I know it's different for you. You're the one in the cast."

Eli nodded.

Eric let go of the curtain and wandered back across the room. He gazed at the posters on the wall before turning his attention back to Eli.

"Listen, I'm trying to help," Eric said. "Tell me what I can do."

"Nothing," Eli said. "I sleep, sometimes. A lot of time I just sit here."

"Is there anything you want? You want a book? Or, I don't know, do you want a movie or something?"

"I don't want anything," Eli said. "I just wish this never happened."

"Me too."

"I wish I could just go back," Eli said.

"Yea," Eric agreed. "I think we all wish that."

"Did you see grandma today?" Eli asked.

"Yea, when your nurse was here I went," Eric said.

"How is she?"

"The same," he said. "Always the same. She still can't move her left side. But she's doing okay. It's just not the same. It's hard seeing her there."

"Does she say anything?"

"Not much. Some stuff, but I think she has a hard time with it. She was really independent. Really strong, ya know?"

Eric leaned against the wall and met Eli's eyes.

"I think about it every day," Eric said. "If I had just. . . If I had just taken her to the hospital, or called 9-1-1, it'd all be different. Maybe she wouldn't even be there. She'd probably be drinking coffee in the kitchen. Things would be the way they're supposed to be."

"But they're not," Eli said.

"No. No, they're not. Everything's messed up," Eric said.

Eric turned and stared blankly at the wall.

"Grandma, you, Cali," he said almost to himself.

Eli started at her name. He looked away from his brother. Why'd he have to say her name?

There was a moment of silence before either was comfortable to say anything more. Eric eventually cleared his throat to speak.

"It'll never be enough, I know that, Eli," he started. "But I am sorry. I'm sorry for everything. For grandma, for Cali, for putting you through this. It's my fault. I'm trying to get better."

"You picked a nice time," Eli spat.

Eric hung his head.

"I know."

"No, you don't understand. Cali is dead. Dead!"

Eli pounded his fist on the bed, pain reverberated through his leg. He howled in agony, writhing and squirming to escape the hurt. With each heartbeat, his broken leg throbbed wretchedly. He pulled a pillow over his head and screamed into it.

His yells turned to sobs as the pain became a dull ache, like an infected tooth.

When Eli pulled his head from his pillow, Eric was gone. That was for the best. There was nothing more to be said right now. He had said enough.

Eli focused on the orange prescription bottle on the bed stand. If only for a little while, the medication would numb him to this impossible reality. He snatched the bottle and popped the two pills in his mouth. He bit down and crunched them. The bitter chalky taste made him gag. But he quickly downed the rest of his water to clean the taste from his tongue. There was a residual bitterness that he couldn't quite get rid of, but soon enough it didn't matter.

The pain in his leg subsided and he felt himself drifting, floating. His face was comfortably warm. His hands seemed cold, but only if he focused on them. If he shifted his focus elsewhere, he didn't notice the cold anymore. He felt light, weightless. His pillows held him afloat. The mental anguish from just a few moments ago seemed distant. It didn't matter anymore. The room was bathed in a warm peaceful glow. There was no need for grief here. There was peace.

Chapter 23

The tree remained. Cali stood beneath it.

The sun was warm on Eli's face as he walked along the small embankment beside the river. The air was hot and dry, perfect for anything, swimming, walking, relaxing. There was an endless expanse of day, ripe with potential, beneath a summer sun. Eli soaked in the warmth, it radiated through his body. A pleasant glow surrounded him, separate from the sun, but just as energizing, a vague force that thrummed through his being. The glow seemed almost a manifestation of his mind. There, but not there. Felt, but not controlled.

Glancing up, he saw Cali waiting. She stood beneath *their tree*, as they had come to know it over this last however long. It felt like forever. Months and years all meshed together in the past like the background in a portrait. The signs were all there, the feelings, the overwhelming sense of familiarity, yet if anyone had ventured to ask Eli precisely when or how long they had visited this tree, the answer would be ambiguous at best. Time was elusory. Sometimes fast, other times slow. Time, especially in the presence of lovers, was not something measured by the ticking of a clock, but by the racing of each heartbeat.

There was no understanding that the past did not exist as Eli remembered it, or less remembered and more felt. Eli felt like he remembered time eternal beneath this tree with Cali. But the truth was not so defined. In fact, time and life itself, were much less stable than Eli imagined.

"I missed you," he said taking Cali in his arms.

She kissed his cheek. Her hair smelled sweet, like almond and honey. He kissed the top of her head and closed his eyes, soaking in the warmth of her embrace.

Though days like this could blur together, there were broad brushstrokes of emotion so vivid they seemed to transcend the individual moment. It wasn't the fact that they sat beneath this tree on this particular day that brought Eli any sort of comfort. Instead it was an overarching feeling he associated with love that seemed to shine especially bright. He had heard it said somewhere, that the days were long, but the years were short. It was probably meant for a different audience, older, wiser. But Eli thought he understood what it meant, or at least, he was finally able to grasp the concept through his own experience. The days did seem long, but never long enough. And as the weeks slipped by, it seemed there was an amalgamated memory of all these individual days, separately together like colors on a canvas, necessary for the larger picture, but specific and unique in their own right. Reds and oranges synonymous with the setting sun were all the brighter because of the blues and purples of the looming night sky. There was a give and take, an understanding that all these things, these colors, these memories, were necessary for the larger picture. Immersed in the moment it was easy not to see the whole scene. Consumed with love, it was easy to forget how equally necessary pain and sadness were.

Eli was lost in the colors, focused on the reds and oranges of this moment, until a splash of blue pulled him away. Cali's tears wet the sleeve of his shirt.

She tried to quickly hide the fact that she was crying. Eli lightly ran his hand through her hair.

"What's wrong?" he asked.

"Nothing," she said.

"Well, it's not nothing, but I won't pry," Eli said.

Cali smiled.

"I miss you," she said.

"I miss you too," Eli replied, wrapping his arms around her and holding her close.

"No, Eli. I really miss you. I miss you so much," Cali said again.

"It's okay," he said. "We're here now. Let's enjoy this."

"This isn't forever though," Cali said. "Eventually, I am going to wake up. I always do. And you won't be there. Eli, I can't do that. I can't."

Eli leaned back to see Cali's eyes. Her bright green eyes starred into his, tears glistened at the corners.

"What do you mean?" Eli asked.

"You wouldn't understand," she said.

"Still, what are you talking about?"

"This, Eli. This. Right now, none of this is real. I know that. But still, I go to bed every night hoping to see you. Hoping that I might be wrong and that this isn't just a dream. But every morning I wake up and you're not there," Cali said.

Her tears glistened in the sunlight as they streamed down her face.

"Cali, that doesn't make sense. I'm right here."

"I know, for now. At least we have the night. That's better than nothing," she said turning her attention to the horizon.

"Cali?"

"You don't need to say anything, just hold me. I don't want to wake up."

They sat down. Eli stretched his legs and sunk deep into a crook at the base of the tree. He leaned back and Cali moved close so her head rested on his chest. Eli mindlessly played with her hair, brooding over Cali's words all the while.

What just happened? What could have been a perfect day was suddenly ruined. Something important had fundamentally changed. If Cali had said she never loved him, as crushing a blow as that might be, there was comfort in the finite. An ending, a relationship over. Brush yourself off and move on. It's never that simple, but in essence that is the outcome of every breakup. Those involved brush themselves off and move on, in some way or other. Either way, there is a path to follow and an understanding of what comes next, even when that path is murky and hidden behind a fog of regret. There is still a path forward. But this conversation had gone somewhere uncharted. There was no path forward, not in any logical sense anyway. Eli could ask more questions, but to what end? What Cali had already said was troubling enough, did he really want to venture further down this rabbit hole, only to find that his girlfriend was going insane? Or, what if Cali was completely lucid and Eli was going crazy? Did he really want to know that? Was it better to assume sanity?

How would someone even recognize if they were losing it? Perception of reality was based on outside influence. If that influence confirmed what you inherently believed, there would be no need to question, right? Maybe he was insane. Maybe he had always been this way. How was he to know?

But no. He felt Cali's head against him. The sweet smell of her hair filled his nostrils. Her gentle breathing and the warmth of her body beside him told him this was not just some fantasy. This was real. All of this was happening. He wasn't crazy. For better or worse, this conversation actually happened.

What then? Was he supposed to just ignore Cali's thoughts? Pretend like nothing had occurred and continue on? That wasn't realistic.

She said, when she wakes up, he isn't there. But what did that even mean?

I go to bed every night hoping to see you, hoping this isn't just a dream.

Cali, what are you trying to say?

Eli shook his head.

Cali had fallen asleep on his chest.

When she woke, what would she think? If this was all just a dream, what was she experiencing now? A dream within a dream? Was he there too, maybe under this same tree? Was he trying to console her and tell her everything was alright? Or did she even cry? Maybe everything was fine and they were enjoying a perfect night.

For a second, Eli felt a pang of jealousy.

It was still a good evening. The sun hadn't said its farewells, there was still so much time. And how much better might this night be because of the conversation they just had? Maybe in some strange way that talk would serve as a catalyst for a brighter discussion? Something more positive. Or maybe not, maybe it would be one of those nights were everything was heavy. Maybe it had to be. Maybe, for whatever reason, this was exactly how things were supposed to be.

Eli frowned. No matter what, something just wasn't sitting right with him. He couldn't spin this situation into something positive. It just wasn't right. But what did she mean? What was she trying to say? None of it made sense. He was only giving himself a headache thinking about it. Best to just let it go.

Eli shifted his hips to stretch his legs. His foot tingled and prickly pain shot through his thigh. It must have fallen asleep he thought. He had sunk low against the tree and a knot in the trunk was now digging into his back. He needed to sit up straight, and let the blood return to his leg. Cali moved with him. She was waking up. She stretched, Eli felt her body tense against him as she yawned. She sat up and rubbed the sleep from her eyes.

She smiled softly.

"I'm still here," Eli said.

Chapter 24

The medication was wearing off. The pain crept up his leg.

Eli opened his eyes. The pill bottle sat on his bed stand. He reached for it and turned the empty bottle over in his hands.

"How's the pain?" Eric asked.

Eli jumped. His brother stepped forward. There was a chair at the end of the bed where he had been sitting. He set a book down on the chair and watched as Eli struggled up to a sitting position.

"How long has it been?" Eli asked.

"Four hours," Eric said.

"That's it?"

"Yea. The pain's coming back?"

Eli set the bottle back on the night stand.

"Yea," he said.

"Wanna try a heating pad on it?" Eric asked.

Eli shrugged. Sleep still had hold of him, though it was slowly relinquishing control.

"Is that supposed to help?" he asked.

"It won't hurt."

Eli eyed his brother.

"Fine. Sure. Let's try it," Eli said.

Eric left the room for a minute and returned with an electric heating pad. He plugged it into the outlet behind the bed stand and laid it across Eli's leg.

"You can adjust it with this button here," he said handing Eli the control.

Eli moved the slider to the hottest setting and leaned back while he waited for it to warm.

"Are there more pain killers?" Eli asked.

Eric stared at the heating pad, but didn't offer an answer.

Eli smiled and shook his head.

"No. No more pain killers. This is supposed to be enough. Right?" he said.

Eric met Eli's eyes.

"Seriously? Eric, Grandma uses this for arthritis," Eli said. "I broke my leg. Come on."

Eric bit his lip and turned his attention to the foot of the bed.

"This is a joke, right?" Eli laughed. "Trust me, the last thing I want is to be like you."

Eric met his younger brother's eyes once more before turning and leaving the room.

"Hey!" Eli yelled as Eric left.

"Eric! Don't leave me like this! Eric!"

There was no answer. Eli sank back in the pillows and sighed. The heating pad was warm, but not nearly enough to ease the pain. He had to think about something else or the agony would never end. He focused on the textured ceiling tiles above. He traced the dots and lines, making images in his mind, but distractions weren't enough to make him forget the pain. Eli ground his teeth.

Eric didn't return.

The white walls were annoyingly bare. Eli wished he had more posters to give him something to look at. Anything would have sufficed right now. As it was, he had two posters, both plain and unexciting. The other walls were undecorated.

There was very little outside stimulus to distract him. He stared at a section of wall, focusing his eyes on one tiny little splotch where the paint hadn't dried smooth. A bubble had formed and below it was a slight crack. His eyes narrowed as he focused on that small inconsistency. The fissure became clear as everything else wavered out of focus. Purple shadows constricted in a strange vignette. Blood rushed to his head. His face felt hot, yet he starred intensely, relishing the peculiar focus similar to the experience of an optical illusion. This was different though, there was almost a feeling of control, such that he had never known. More of his peripheral vision shifted to purple and black as he focused ever more intensely. The fissure seemed to magnify in his eyes and as it grew larger, the distance between himself and the wall shrank. Space shifted, or better, Eli felt the air around him thicken, like walking through fog after an evening rain. The fracture opened, and Eli peered into the abyss. Darkness and shifting shadows greeted him. But in the dark, Eli spied movement. There was something on the other side, voices, laughter. He drew closer. The slit opened wide, darkness turned to light and he saw clearly.

Like a mirror's reflection, there was a room with a bed. In it, he saw two people, a girl and boy, holding fast to one another. Their bodies entwined in a loving embrace. The covers hid them from view. The blood rushed to Eli's face. He was seeing something he was not invited to, something he shouldn't be seeing. But there was a familiarity to it, to this scene. He knew it. He could feel it. He had felt that touch, he had known what it was like to be with another person and let the day pass. Time was irrelevant, just the beating of hearts and the exciting tension of a hesitant kiss. Then a little more. The tension growing with each movement, each touch of hands. Their bodies moved together in a dance, a symphony, perfectly timed, hesitant at first, but with each step, each movement, their song became stronger and more deliberate. Like water rushing toward a fall, gaining speed and power, there was no turning back. There was no desire to, this felt right, this was the way it was supposed to be.

Eli felt all this, more than saw. There was little to see. He was partly ashamed for looking in the first place. Yet, there was a part of him that understood the scene better for not seeing. There was a feeling inside him that resonated with this moment, that could feel all the tension in every touch. The blood coursed hot beneath his skin. He lived this moment. This was not just a memory, some passing glimpse of a time before. He felt it all. Better than any dream, it was like he had slipped back into this moment and was experiencing it all again for the first time.

And yet, there was a distinct separation. He was there, but he was not there. Like having a conversation, but thinking about something else. Eli felt everything, but he wasn't there. He knew he wasn't there. But still, it felt so real.

Perhaps this was his own memory. And maybe that's why it felt real. But you couldn't physically feel memories. You could remember how something felt, but that wasn't the same as actually feeling it. And that's what he experienced, actual feeling. The gentle touch of her fingers on his hand and through his hair, her lips against his, the warmth of her body nestled against him. That was real. But how?

He felt himself slipping. Sliding back through the crevice and to his bed. The room opened up before him once more. The pain in his leg jumped to the forefront of his mind. The thoughts and feelings so prominent only a second ago seemed to fade to the background. Here was reality. This was real. The pain was real. The barren room in which he resided was real.

Whatever he had seen through the wall, wasn't. At least, not in the same way. Still, he couldn't shake the feeling of her touch. He glanced at his hand. He felt the lingering pressure of her fingers squeezing his. On the other side of the wall was something real, he couldn't explain how. It was something felt, not really understood. Much of life worked that way. Feelings and emotions overpowered facts.

The truth was that Cali was dead. Eli knew this. He had been told this. He had gradually come to accept it. But what he felt was something different. Cali wasn't dead. He couldn't explain it and he knew if he tried, they, Eric or doctors or anyone willing to listen to him, would think he was crazy. Maybe he was. He couldn't change what he felt, and what he felt, seemed more real than the truth. The truth was cold and unyielding. What he felt, was warm and comforting. And he preferred that.

Chapter 25

So, it was that Eli spent much of that afternoon waiting. Watching and wondering about the small crack in the wall. A crack unnoticed before now consumed his every thought. What had he really seen and felt? He stared closely, waiting for a sign, anything that might tell him he wasn't as crazy as he felt. That one section of wall consumed him. He focused hard and then relaxed his eyes. There was some trick to it, something he had done unconsciously at first. He tried to open the fissure again, but to no avail. The secrets of the other side were to remain hidden from Eli or so it seemed after hours of fruitless staring.

All the while his mind was at work. What had he seen? It was something more than a dream, but less than reality. It was some sort of middle ground between what was and what could be. He had seen something, so it stood to reason that there was something. Or at least, that was his conclusion. There was something on the other side of the wall, a mirror world. A world where Cali was still alive.

She was with him there. If only he could be with her.

Eli contemplated what he had seen and felt. It seemed impossible. There was no such thing as a mirror world, some perfect parallel universe.

It would be easier if he could just forget that he saw anything. He tried. He tried to tell himself it was all a dream, or maybe a hallucination. He tried to focus his attention elsewhere, but his eyes were constantly drawn back to that small imperfection. He knew it couldn't be real. Yet, he felt her touch. He felt her hand in his.

There was no getting around that. Just, it was hard to conceive or accept.

He knew this was the sort of wishful thinking found in romance movies. The sort of dauntless optimism that encouraged people to believe it would all be okay, because no one was really ever gone. The thought made him shudder, and still, here he was willing to suspend disbelief if it gave him what he wanted. Cali wasn't gone. At least not in the mirror world.

If only he could open the wall once more. If he could see through it again. If he could take her hand in his once more, maybe then he would know the truth. But knowing wouldn't be enough. If he could see through to this other world and he could feel Cali's touch, why couldn't he just step through the wall completely? Why couldn't he just step into another life where Cali was still alive?

But then, what would happen? If he could really step into that existence, what would happen to his body? He couldn't be in two places at once, so what would happen to him? Would he cease to exist here? How would that even work? And then what about the other Eli? He couldn't just take over someone else's life.

It was all useless. It was no more real than a dream. But still. He had seen something. A dream or a reflection of life. His life. He was the same person. There or here, it was him either way, right? He was the person with Cali, but he was also the person here in his bed mourning his dead girlfriend. He was the boy who wrecked his grandmother's car and killed his best friend. He was that boy. Did his life beyond the wall have the same struggles? Maybe not at the moment but somewhere, sometime soon, would he deal with the same situation?

If the mirror world existed, did the Eli in that world also suffer the same tragic flaws? Did that version of himself spend most of his summer dreaming of a future with no commitments or restrictions, a future where time was nothing?

Eli's thoughts wandered. He remembered his talks with Cali. She had plans, she had a future laid out. She was going to do something with her life. She was going to, until the accident. She had plans, until she died. Tears welled at the corners of his eyes. He should have been the one to die, not Cali. He was just hitching a ride with her. Cali had a future. Eli was a loser. She was going places, and Eli would have gone with her, as long as she wanted him there.

I didn't deserve it, Eli thought. I didn't deserve to be with Cali, she deserved someone so much better.

How long would she have wanted him by her side, anyway? She would outgrow him in college. That was a certainty. He might make it through a semester, maybe two, but he would fail out. She would make the Dean's list. She would make her parents proud. But as she moved up in the world, she would leave him behind. Like a favorite shirt that didn't fit anymore, Eli would fall by the wayside. It would happen slowly. She wouldn't want to leave him, but it would happen. Over time she would realize her own potential. She had already noticed Eli's lack of ambition. Why would she want to stay with him? He wasn't going anywhere. He would just hold her back. He was deadweight.

Eli dreamed of a future. It was always just dreaming, though. There were no plans as to how to get there, just dreams. Dreams of some magical future, with no problems, no pain or suffering, just peace and love. An impossible journey without a plan.

Would that be his life? Empty dreams that never amounted to anything? Was he doomed to be some helpless romantic that never realized his own potential? What potential? He wasn't smart, not smart enough anyway. He wasn't bound for college. He wasn't athletic. Not really. He wasn't particularly handsome. He couldn't skate through life on good looks alone. He was really about as middle the road as you could get. He was hopelessly average. Cali had been the one exception to his life. Now what?

He ran his hand over his forehead and through his hair. His mind was racing. Pain radiated in his forehead and to his temples. He couldn't keep thinking. Not like this. It would drive him crazy. But he didn't have an outlet. Eric was gone. He hadn't been here for some time. There was no one to listen. He was alone.

He glanced at his bed stand. A notebook lay buried under a litany of miscellaneous items. He pulled the book out from under the debris. A pen fell to the floor as well as some loose scraps of paper. Eli leaned over the edge of the bed, stretching and nearly falling, and just barely grasped the pen. He sat back up, the blood rushed from his head. His face grew warm and his head spun for a second.

He opened the notebook; the first page was blank. Eli couldn't remember when he had gotten the book or why. It didn't matter. There was a use for it now. He needed an outlet, a pressure release valve.

Although, he didn't really know where to begin. Should he start before the accident or after? What did he really want to say?

Again, it didn't matter. This wasn't a story with a beginning and an end, not in some idealized way. This was his life, this moment in time. What he wrote didn't matter so much as the fact that he wrote something.

Eli put pen to paper and felt the words flow from him. The pen became a sort of magician's wand releasing every feeling, thought, and memory that was locked up in his mind. One page filled and then another and another. An endless stream of thoughts poured forth upon the page. It wasn't grammatically sound writing, not in the least. None of it would make much sense to anyone else. It was an assortment of thoughts and feelings, observations and longings. Everything that he was trying to organize in his mind was spewed upon the page, there for him to see.

When he set his pen down, he felt relieved, lighter even. He didn't have an answer for anything yet. The pages were riddled with questions, probably even more questions than Eli realized he had. But there was something to be said for seeing his problems laid out in this way. Just being written down seemed to give his thoughts room to breathe.

He smiled.

Chapter 26

"Eli, come on," Cali called from the river.

He walked down the embankment, the grass brushed against his knee brace as he descended. The sweet smell of summer, hot air and sunshine, filled his nose. The sun's warmth radiated through him. It made him feel full, alive. He was strong, there wasn't any pain in his leg. Not for a while now.

Time seemed a blur. There were memories of rehab, of rebuilding the muscle around his femur, the muscles that had atrophied after the accident. But the pain of regrowth was gone, he felt good now. He probably didn't even need the brace.

The embankment smoothed flat with only a slight tilt toward the river's edge. Cali was already on the rocks. She leaned on a walking stick, her back to the river. She watched Eli navigate the cattails that grew close to the water.

Reeds that grew thick by the river hid much. The ground was tricky, hollow tufts of earth could give way to thick soupy sludge. It wasn't a problem normally. Eli knew the steps.

Cali's eyes drifted to the brace on his leg. One misstep could ruin months of rehabilitation.

Eli followed Cali's footprints. They had traversed this path so often; the steps were engrained in his mind. He stepped right, then left, over the soft tussocks and past a small puddle of water, the remnant of a pool formed separate from the river after a rainstorm a while back. The ground squinched beneath his foot. He nearly slipped once, as a soft spot gave way beneath him. In a moment though, he emerged from the rushes and onto the smooth stones that lined the river's edge beneath the bridge.

Cali beamed. She reached out her hand and Eli took it. They walked on, into the cool midday shadows under the bridge. Sunlight sparkled on the water, creating a shimmering surface for them to look upon. The river's song filled their ears; gently lapping water splashed over rocks, along the shore, beneath downed trees and branches that dotted the river sporadically. Dancing to its own cadence, the river lulled the teens into an easy peace. They found on old log, washed ashore from a previous storm upon which to sit. Eli borrowed Cali's stick to lower himself onto the seat.

Once settled, the two leaned against each other.

As the sun moved across the summer sky, its rays reflected upon the water, Eli noticed a subtle change in their color. Subtle, like the emergence of stars on a clear night, the sunlight shifted from a bright-hot white to a sweet, soft, amber glow. Maybe it only really changed in his mind. The difference was so slight, he couldn't be sure it actually happened. It was more of a feeling, like he felt the color.

He let the light wash over him. The golden hue became brighter, taking on a presence of its own. The light seemed to grow thicker, becoming dense like fog. Yet, Eli could see through it. Sort of like a film or a pair of tinted glass, it cast an orangish glow. The light flowed through the air, between Eli and Cali, over the river, through the trees. Unencumbered by physical form, the light seemed to drift over and through everything. Its soothing touch was warm and comforting.

Eli leaned his head against Cali's and let the moment fill him with an untouchable happiness.

Moments ago, the blinding bright sun was unyieldingly hot. But now, it felt like a warm embrace, a comfortable heat, open and free, unrestricting.

Sometime later, Eli woke to the sound of a piercing metallic scraping outside. He sat up in bed, the light of his dream still clouding his eyes. He pulled the curtains in his window aside and saw one of the neighbors pulling some sort of tin roofing sheet behind a bicycle. A rope tied to the bike's frame was looped through a hole in the tin. As the man rode slowly by, the grating sound of tin on cement was like a knife in Eli's ears.

"What the hell?" he said as he collapsed back on his pillow. The sounds seemed to cut through the air, nails on a chalkboard didn't do it justice. Its harshness was equaled only by its unending discord. The grinding cacophony continued on, dolling out its treachery moment by moment, until finally, it seemed to disappear in the distance. For some time after, the memory of that horrid grating sounded in Eli's ears.

As he sat in bed, waiting for the discordant noise to evaporate, Eli tried to focus on anything else. The few posters he had on the wall were of little appeal. The small crack that had consumed him not that long ago, was hard to focus on with the clanging in his ears. Instead he closed his eyes and tried to imagine the details of his dream.

The sun, warm on his skin, was easy enough to recall. The sweet scent of the grass came back to him. There was the river too. After a few moments, the splashing of water over rocks, crisp and clear, returned to him, deadening the sound of that wretched grating.

Then she was there. Beautiful as he remembered. Her bright green eyes dazzled in the summer light. Light freckles on her cheeks came to life in the sun. Cali smiled, her face aglow with a light from within. She glistened in the noontime light.

The image of her existed, untarnished in Eli's mind. She was perfect beyond compare, beyond beauty. Cali was something more. She embodied summer, the light, the warmth, the freedom. Freedom. Cali was free. In a way, she was freer now than in life.

Eli opened his eyes. He blinked, her image was blazed on the back of his eyelids. Her glow remained for a second as his eyes became accustomed to the relative dark of his room again.

He picked up his notebook and pencil. He was never a great artist. He didn't really know how to make the picture he wanted. But there was an image in his mind and he had time. He opened the notebook and flipped past his writing from earlier. He didn't want to draw where he was writing, so he flicked to the back. His heart stopped when he saw the last page. It was her. Cali. He had drawn her picture before. He touched the lines of her face with his fingertips. The drawing was from before the accident. Almost identical to the image from his dream.

Eli turned the page and another picture met his eyes. A forgotten dream came to life. An old gnarled hand held a woodworker's chisel. And as he gazed at the image, he felt the smooth wooden handle in his palm and smelled the fragrant air of the shop. He shook his head. It was just a drawing. But the memories were something more.

He flipped to an empty page and set to work recording his memory, his dream, whichever it may be. Light pencil strokes became a gray base. Darker lines accentuated her beauty. The image came to life with each layer of gray. Despite the lack of color, Eli saw her as he remembered. On the page her eyes were shades of gray, but to Eli, they were bright green as he remembered. She would never change.

Memories blazed brighter than the sun, glimpses of the truth. Cali was beautiful, that was true. Had she grown old and time worn away the shallow beauty of her body, she would have still been beautiful, Eli knew that. Her beauty wasn't in the gleam of her hair or the softness of her skin. Those things were temporary. Her beauty was much deeper than that, it was a feeling that emanated from her, a feeling of warmth and joy. She was summer. And would always be summer.

That beauty might have faded beneath the wears of time if she had lived longer. Beneath a lifetime of experience, maybe she would have changed. Maybe pain or regrets would wear on her and harden her heart. Maybe life would take that youthful joy from her, sapping her of that perfect splendor and leaving her old and feeble and sad and bitter. But that wasn't her. It wasn't her fate. She was forever to be beautiful. Forever free. There was truth in that sort of beauty. Where life tarnished beauty and destroyed the nature of someone like Cali, memories of their true being persisted. Memories in the lives they touched. That was truth.

Eli set his pencil down and looked at the page. It was her. It was her, truly. All that it lacked was the dimension of realism, the ability to touch and talk, to move and exist apart from the page. That only came with life. But that wasn't totally true, Eli thought. He had seen and felt something as real as life. Something more than a drawing, but just as true.

Cali was alive.

Chapter 27

When Eli set his pencil to the side, his eyes were stinging and heavy. Determined to finish the drawing, he powered through his body's cries for sleep. Now finished, his eyelids slipped closed, the last image blazed in his mind. Cali.

The heavy clang of a bell sounded in the distance.

"Eli, wake up," Cali said.

Was this all they did? Sleep?

Cali materialized before his eyes, or maybe he blinked the sleep away. Either way, she was before him. Her hand in his, she pulled him from the bed. Eli stumbled across the room behind her.

All was dark.

Eli reached for the light switch, but Cali stayed his hand.

"They are here," she whispered.

"Who? What's going on?" he tried to ask.

Cali covered his mouth, muffling his words.

"Just follow my lead," she said.

She slipped through the doorway, Eli close behind. The room beyond was just as dark as the last, all shadows upon shadows. Cali moved quick, effortlessly gliding through the room, Eli struggled to keep up.

Cali darted around a corner, or at least she stepped to the right around something, some pillar or wall. Eli's hand slipped free. In his haste to keep up he slammed into something. There was a loud screech as whatever he hit scrapped across the floor. Eli tripped, the chair or desk, whatever it was crashed beside him in a deafening blast.

"Eli!" Cali screamed up ahead.

Eli scrambled to his feet just in time to feel a cold breeze rush past him. Footsteps echoed off the walls. Heavy and wet, they squelched past.

"Hey!" Eli called out.

He ran. The person before him hurried onward, the clapping slap of their feet sounded louder and faster.

Eli gave chase, but the hall was still dark, he couldn't tell how far ahead the person was.

Cali screamed. Her cry was cut short, her voice stifled.

"Hey! Leave her be!" Eli yelled as he raced down the hall.

"Leave her be! Don't touch her!"

The hallway grew deathly quiet.

"Cali! Cali!"

His heart pounded in his chest as he ran faster. But the hall stretched on endlessly. The walls closed around him. Still he ran. Cali had to be close.

Then suddenly, the hall flashed brilliant white, like a lightning strike during a summer storm. Eli froze, the sudden illumination shot through his eyes, subduing him with blinding pain. He collapsed.

"Cali!" he cried out. His voice distant in his own ears. "Cali, where are you?"

He shielded his eyes with his hand.

He heard Cali's voice echo on the horizon, her words like the last vestiges of a memory, barely audible and fading fast.

"No! Cali, I'm here!" he rose to his feet, his hand still covering his eyes.

"Cali!"

He started down the hall once more. The passage became narrow. Everything was white, terribly bright and uniform. Peeking through the gaps of his fingers, Eli though he could discern some sort of soft material along the walls. But it was hard to tell.

He scrambled forward keeping his eyes on the grey floor beneath him. The hall would end eventually and he would find Cali. He had to. So, he lumbered on.

But the hallways seemed to stretch on forever. There was no end, just more of the same. White walls and grey floors blending together to a perfect union, bleeding into each other. The colors melted to one vast shade of gray.

Then, he saw something.

At the edge of nothing, she appeared. Emerging from out of the gray, her dark skin pulled the hues of white from the surrounding area and gave her an unnatural pallor.

Eli ran, removing his hand from over his eyes to see her better, regardless of the pain. A mist formed round her legs and hid her feet. Cali seemed to float above the floor, holding steady in the air before him as the ground beneath disappeared to nothing.

He stepped forward. Solid ground became white gray sky beneath his feet. It was soft but firm under the weight of his foot. Eli stepped out further, Cali waited for him. A smile played at the corner of her lips, ushering him on.

Step by step, he drew closer. Cali remained fixed before him. Then, just as he reached out to take her hands, she changed. Her jaw dropped as a painful scream erupted from her lips. Her eyes rolled back in her head.

A dark stain trailed from her mouth down her jaw and neck. Her scream died away to silence as her head lolled forward.

Eli reached for her, but she slipped through his hands and faded in the mists below. Eli collapsed. The mists swallowed him.

The image of her dying face burned his eyes.

He shot awake.

Cali's face starred up at him, her head in his lap. Startled, Eli covered her face with his hands, but he quickly realized it was only his notebook. The dream was over. He folded the notebook closed.

But then, a thought came to him. He opened the book again and grabbed the pen from his bed stand. He flipped to an empty page and wrote down the details of his dream, as best as he could recall, before they disappeared for good. The images were fading fast, but as Eli recorded his dream, writing down in detail all he could remember, he breathed life into emptiness and turned a fuzzy image into a memory.

The word written down served as a gateway. As with most dreams, the images would have faded, but now, there was something to hold on to. Fleeting as the dream was, it now lived stronger in Eli's mind. As he read over his writing, he felt his heart race as though he was living the dream once more.

He smiled and closed his notebook for now.

Chapter 28

That night and for the next several days, Eli recorded his dreams in his notebook. With each entry, he gained a stronger memory of his dreams. The first couple days Eli would wake in the morning or after a nap and jot down his dream. But as time wore on, he began to wake after each sleep cycle. He would flutter awake in the middle of the night and try to describe his dream in his notebook. He would wake in the morning to find his previous entry scribbled on the page, for the most part still legible.

One day, as he read his entry from the night before, Eli was startled by the clarity with which the dream returned to his memory. The words were scrambled and lacked any cogency apart from his memory, but the fact that he could draw meaning from midnight ramblings provided an odd sort of comfort. Comfort he desperately craved.

His dreams became more and more the highlight of each passing day. He struggled to move, even with crutches. The bone wasn't healing like the doctors had hoped, and Eli was growing restless with his limited mobility. There were times when the pain was still excruciating. For the most part though, Eli resided in a sort of purgatory where the dull ache in his leg refused to subside, but wasn't painful enough to require medication. Besides, Eric was keeping a close eye on the narcotics.

There was no TV. He had already read the few books he owned and the pile of magazines his brother had given him. So, his only escape became his dreams.

He spent the days dreaming of sleep, where Cali was more than just a memory.

He read over his latest entry and then closed his eyes, letting the memory materialize. Cali emerged from the dark, her familiar smile perfect in every way. She extended her hand, lightly brushing Eli's with her fingertips.

Eli took her hand and squeezed gently. Here was a truth to her touch, her skin was warm and soft in his hand. As real as life.

Then the dream faded and Eli was thrust back to reality.

"Are you going or not?" Eric's voice came from the hall.

Eli turned to the sound.

"Where?"

"Come on, I'm not going through it all again," Eric said.

He stepped into the room and extended a hand to Eli.

"The wheelchair is downstairs, I'll help ya down."

"I can use the crutches."

"I know you can."

"Where are we going?"

"Therapy."

Chapter 29

"Eli, this only works if you talk to me," Dr. Guevait said.

"I am talking to you."

"Yes, you are," the doctor nodded.

Then, there was silence.

Dr. Guevait glanced out the window, blue skies and a few happy clouds greeted him.

"Beautiful day," he said.

"Yep," Eli replied turning his attention outside as well.

After a couple minutes of silence, the doctor closed his notebook.

"We are closing in on an hour, we can call it a day. I'll see you again next week," he said.

Eli nodded and rolled toward the door.

Eli's hand rested on the handle when Dr. Guevait called him.

"Eli, I meant to ask, you're getting plenty of sleep, right?"

Eli turned.

"What?"

"Sleep. Are you having trouble sleeping? You look tired, I didn't know if the pain in your leg was keeping you up," Dr. Guevait said.

"Yea, no, I'm good."

"Alright, well, take care. We'll see you next week."

"Yea, next week."

Eli rolled out of the room. Eric was waiting in a chair down the hall. He stood up when Eli rolled near.

"Ready?"

"Yea, let's go," Eli said.

It was silent in the car as they drove. Eli picked at the fabric of his pants overtop his cast. He caught glimpses of Eric watching him, waiting for him to say something. But he wouldn't. He bit his lip. It wouldn't help to say anything, it would only aggravate him. He could feel Eric's eyes on him though, searching for an answer, some sign he had done the right thing. That his younger brother was healing, or somehow coping with the loss of his girlfriend. How could Eli explain to him? He wasn't alright. Therapy was a waste of time, an hour of silence with someone he didn't know or want to know. What did Eric want? Smiles, great big sighs of relief. Thanks? Thanks for taking me to the shrink, for having my head cracked and investigated. Maybe if someone could just take a look at his brain, splattered all over the wall they could find out what's wrong.

There was nothing wrong. How could Eric understand anyway? Even if something was wrong, how would he understand? He couldn't. No one could.

They all tried to tell him the same thing, Eric, the doctor, the therapist. They all said it would take time, time to heal, time to accept, time to forget. But he didn't want to forget. He couldn't. She was always here, when he closed his eyes, there she was, true as a blue sky.

They wouldn't understand because they couldn't see her like he could. They didn't know.

"What?" he said finally, breaking the awkward silence.

"What?" Eric said simply.

"I asked you," Eli said.

"It was more of a statement, I don't know what you're asking," Eric said.

"What do you want, why do you keep looking at me?"

Eric turned his eyes to Eli, his brow furrowed in question.

"I'm driving, Eli. I'm not looking at you."

"Stop. You do to," Eli said.

"Do what?" Eric asked.

"Never mind," Eli said as he turned to the passenger window and watched the trees pass.

He didn't care anyways. If he didn't have to explain himself to Eric, all the better. He just wanted to sleep. It took a lot to travel anywhere or to do anything. It would get easier, they said, once his leg healed. He wasn't holding his breath though. Part of him believed he would be walking with a limp from now on. Once he started walking anyway.

They pulled into the parking lot of the Athletic Sports Rehab building. Eric helped Eli out of the car and they went inside. It was hot and sticky. The place smelled of sweat and bleach.

His trainer met them at the door and took them to a side room, away from the main gym.

"So how do you feel?" she asked.

"Fine," Eli answered.

"Good, that's good. We have a bit yet before we can actually start working on your rehab. Once the caste comes off, then we will be able to do more. Right now, there are some things, small things you can do to help strengthen those muscles though, okay?" she said.

Eli nodded.

She took him through a couple exercises and Eli followed her directions. He was more accepting of the help here than at the psych's office. He couldn't say why. Maybe it was the movement. Not being stuck sitting or lying down. Maybe because it felt like learning to walk would bring him back to some sense of normalcy. He wanted to do something. He just didn't want to talk.

When they left, he was in better spirits. Eric bought lunch at a fast food place and they drove home. There were worse ways to spend the day. This would be better once the cast was off, he thought. He looked forward to that day. But the rehab specialist said it was still a long and arduous journey back.

"Arduous," he said.

Eric grunted, a mouthful of burger preventing him from saying more.

"It's never a medium journey is it?" Eli asked.

"What?"

"The journey. The trainer, she said it was an arduous journey."

"Right?"

"So, there are only two types of journeys, arduous and easy," Eli said. "No one talks about the easy ones, I guess cause there isn't much to say. But the arduous ones, they get all the focus."

"Okay, not sure where you're going with this, but I think I follow you," Eric said.

"There's no middle ground, like there's no medium fries' type of journeys," Eli said taking a couple fries in his mouth. "Like the burger place doesn't sell only small and large fries. But they should.

Medium is the feel-good place for people who want large, but know they are fine with small."

He ate another fry.

"But you got medium," Eric said.

Eli smiled.

"Yea, I did."

They drove on in silence for a few minutes as Eli collected his thoughts.

"Okay, it's like this, there is no medium because we hyperbolize everything," Eli said.

"I like that, we hyperbolize everything," Eric said.

"Right. Like everything is the best or the worst," Eli said. "That movie is the best, that one is trash. Or food is amazing or crap. No one talks about the middle, the movie with the gapping plot holes but entertaining story. That gets lost in the conversation. No one talks about the burger that's alright, it's either the best or so bad you would rather eat dog turds."

Eric laughed.

"I think the truth is closer to the middle, it's not the best or the worst, it's usually just medium," he said. "I think most journeys aren't actually that arduous, we just don't know how to say it's a medium level journey."

"I like that analysis," Eric said.

"Yea?"

"Seriously, not bad considering you've had to ride around all afternoon with me," Eric said. "It's nice to have some thoughtful commentary, even if it's about burgers and fries and adventures."

"That'll be the name of my movie, 'Burgers, Fries and the Great Medium Adventure,'" Eli laughed.

"I'll watch it," Eric said with a smile.

They pulled up to the house and finished their lunch. Eli threw his hamburger wrapper in the to-go bag and turned to his brother.

"I haven't asked, but how's the baby?" Eli said.

Eric wiped his mouth and smiled.

"The baby is gonna be alright," he said. "Early tests weren't accurate and the baby is developing just fine."

"And is she…" Eli left off.

"She's good. We're talking and we'll see what happens. But things seem good right now," Eric said.

"That's good," Eli said.

"Yea, it's gonna be alright. Come on, let's go," Eric said as he opened his door.

He helped Eli up the stairs to his room. Once there, Eli settled into bed. With his notebook open on his lap, he read his latest dream entry. Words mixed with memory. He struggled to keep his eyes open. The littlest tasks were exhausting, and it had been a busy day. It wasn't more than a few minutes before his eyes closed and he slipped back into that other realm.

Chapter 30

"Why are we here?" Eli asked.

Cali shushed him with a wave of her hand. She pointed toward a small fracture in the paint and motioned Eli closer.

He obliged. This wasn't what he wanted. Starring at a wall, waiting for something, but he would follow Cali to the end of the Earth. So, he moved closer.

Cali urged him to look at the small crack and he did. It was like looking through a keyhole into another room. Through the fissure in the wall, Eli saw what looked to be a bedroom. Plain white walls, a non-descript bed, a night stand and dresser. The room beyond was quaint and simple.

He stepped back and shrugged his shoulders.

"I don't understand what is this?" he whispered.

Cali pointed at the small hole in the wall again, her eyes fixed on Eli, her jaw set.

Eli sighed and looked again. This time he saw it. There was someone in the bed. He squinted, trying to see better. The person seemed to be sleeping. As Eli took in the scene, the hair on his neck rose and a chill raced down his spine.

He knew the room and the person.

He stepped away from the wall and turned to Cali. A buzzing rang in his ears. She grinned.

"Eli," she said softly as she took his hands.

He met her eyes. He knew what she wanted to say, but he put his finger to her lips. Do not say it, he thought. Do not, should the mere speaking of a thing make it dissolve before his eyes and break the spell. It was enough that he knew. If she knew also, that was just as well for now.

Like a child skipping along a sidewalk cautious of avoiding every crack, Eli refused to say what he acknowledged to be true. As if words alone could destroy.

Yet with this knowledge a world was now open. A door that had been closed now opened revealing a perfect paradise. All they ever wanted was theirs for the taking.

Eli smiled and leaned close to Cali. Their lips met.

When he opened his eyes, he was once again in his bedroom. But that didn't come with the same defeated feeling as it normally did. There was a secret knowledge upon which he could now act. He wrote his dream in his notebook, his hands couldn't record the details fast enough. He had stumbled upon a truth, and he needed to write it all down. A gateway was opened and Eli had the key.

Chapter 31

"Eli, you need to move," Eric said.

"I know," Eli said through gritted teeth.

"Grandma's coming home today. Are you gonna stay up here?"

"I'll be down."

"No, I'm gonna go down the stairs with you. Grandma isn't gonna want to see you rolling on the floor like a turtle on its back, first thing as she walks in the door," Eric said.

"I'll be fine."

"Right, let's go," Eric held out his arm.

Eli snapped his notebook closed and wriggled to the side of the bed and took Eric's arm. He barely put pressure on his leg, most of his weight was held by Eric. They moved through the room and to the top of the stairs.

"I got it," Eli said as he reached for the bannister to steady himself.

"I'll be a couple steps ahead of you," Eric said.

Eli nodded.

Then he hopped down a step, all the pressure on his good leg, his broken limb just barely touching the carpeted step. He inched his hand down the railing and hopped down again, then again, all the way.

He stopped to rest at the bottom step, panting but smiling.

"Every step," he said through ragged breaths.

"You're getting better."

Eli hobbled across the room and collapsed on the couch. Gazing out the front window, he saw some kids fly past on bikes. They sped up the street and skid

...ertop gravel, swerving to make long marks along the side of the road.

He smiled. But there was no joy in his face, only longing.

Eric wandered to the front door and gazed down the street. After a time, he turned to his brother. He opened his mouth to say something, but stopped himself. He went to the kitchen and returned with two cups of coffee a minute later.

"Here," he said as he sat next to Eli.

Eli took the cup and thanked Eric. Neither said anything else while they sipped their coffee. They just watched the street and the monotonous routines of other residents through the front window.

"What do you think?" Eli asked after some time.

"I try not to," Eric said. Eli turned and met his brother's eyes. Eric smiled softly, a real smile. Eli smiled back. Then, he turned his attention back outside and his expression shifted.

Eric saw the change. There was pain and struggle behind his brother's forlorn gaze. Eric had lived that struggle side by side with Eli. He was there in the hospital the day it happened and every day thereafter. He watched his brother's motionless body for days. Back then, at the hospital, no one really knew if Eli would make it. In some ways the question remained. Could Eli continue on? Recovery is a long road and there were plenty of hurdles beyond physical limitations. Eric was doing his best to guide Eli along, to bring him back. As iron sharpens iron, so one man sharpens another. But it remained to be seen if Eli could stand against the heat of the furnace.

For now, there was something to celebrate. Eric stood and stretched deep. He drained the last of his coffee. Eli glanced down at his mug, still more than half full.

"When are you leaving to get her?" he asked.

"Soon," Eric replied.

"Did you want me to go?"

"That's up to you, boss," Eric said.

"Then, I'm going to stay," Eli said.

"Alright," Eric nodded as he strode across the room to the front door. "Just be careful."

"I'm not going anywhere," Eli said.

"I mean, just try not to do too much, you're still healing."

Eli chuckled. "Eric, I'm not going anywhere."

He sank into the couch.

Eric wandered out to the kitchen. Eli held his coffee in his lap while he listlessly watched the street. There was action, or movement anyway. People going about their days such as they were, smoking on porch steps, berating their children, or shuffling through junk piled on front yards. Everyone was busy doing something, but no one was really living.

Eric said something as he stepped outside. Eli didn't register it.

He stared, his eyes taking in the street beyond the door, a world unto itself. A figure moved among the human debris. Lithe and smooth, contrasted with the clumsy meanderings of everyone else. A goddess, walking the streets alone. The peasants parting ways to clear a path. She moved with purpose.

It was only a dream.

Eli stood, there was no pain. He walked to the open door and greeted Cali with a kiss. She wrapped her arms around him.

It was only a dream, Eli knew, but it felt good.

He hugged her back and ushered her inside; the living room shifted and spread wide before them. The murmured voices of guests cloistered against the walls, provided a warm thrum. They glided through the room to the center of the dancefloor, the diamond chandelier above reflected the emerald green of Cali's dress. Hungry eyes, watched the two with rapt attention. But no one else meant a thing at this moment, just Cali.

Eli waved his hand, the band was somewhere, they would take his cue. The trumpet came in first, a heavy drumbeat followed. And they were off. The music took hold and the floor filled with dancers. A sultry voice whispered into a microphone and mingled with the sound of shuffling feet.

Though there was a crowd, no one disturbed Eli and Cali. They danced and moved effortlessly across the room. Other dancers may have been on the floor. . . No one missed a step, no one interfered, it was a perfect symphony of bodies in motion.

A haze formed at the edge of the room. Eli noticed it and his heart sank. They had only just begun, it couldn't be over already. But it was only a dream.

He fought the waves of time. They lapped against the shore of life, a rhythmic pounding like some doom drum signaling the end.

He spun, ignoring the haze and focusing all his attention on Cali. This moment couldn't end. He wouldn't let it. They twirled through the crowd, Cali's dress a whirl of green. Her cheek was pressed to Eli's.

"Don't let me go," she whispered.

"Never."

The haze drew closer, dimming the periphery and reminding Eli he didn't have the luxury of forever. This was only a dream.

"I miss you, Eli," Cali said, her hand firm along his side. "You should be here."

She turned her face. Eli felt her choke back tears as he held her. What was he to say? The truth didn't matter, this was only a dream. The truth wouldn't change this moment. He kissed her lightly on the cheek. Her tears wet his lips.

The haze constricted. This was the end. Hours condensed to minutes. They had danced this way before. But how many times? He couldn't recall. Golden rays of memory were overlaid with the sound of jazz and Cali's voice in his ear.

He smiled. The haze had come to them now. It always did. Cali, pressed tight against him, but even she started to blur as the haze consumed everything. Eli smiled anyway. It was only a dream, but it was a good one.

He blinked, the mid-day sun shined upon the dead-end street beyond the front door. There was something firm about the street. Something he couldn't quite place. Maybe it was the mundane? The monotony of a moment he didn't control. He couldn't fix this scene. He couldn't change the people, or the environment. They were here whether he liked it or not. Their lives would continue on for years the same as they always had, the same as they always would. Maybe that was the feeling he couldn't place. That sort of existence out of time or because of time. These people would keep on keeping on, even if Eli were gone. If he left for a hundred years and came back, the scene would be about the same. Maybe a little changed, different faces, but for the most part it would remain the same depressing street in the same depressing town.

It was so far removed from the dreams he had, so vivid and lively. There was a life worth living. Not this squabbling, rat-trap of an existence fighting over pennies, for a little bit of scrap to be sold in an antique store for a pack of smokes. This life was junk piled atop junk forever. His dream was a taste of class, a taste of what life should be. True happiness encapsulated in a moment, a kiss, a touch. That was truth. All this, the fighting in the streets, that was the dream, a nightmare.

He sipped his coffee, it was still warm.

Chapter 32

She wasn't the same. Her smile was gone, only a shadow remained. Her voice was weak. She looked frail and diminished. She wasn't even a shell of her former self. The elderly woman that returned from the nursing home was skin and bones, a broken-down husk of a body. Her soul was gone. The essence of her being now eroded away and what was left was a withered head on the vine. She clung to life, but she was dead in every way.

Eric catered to the feeble woman, but no amount of food and drink, or warmth and comfort, could revive the parts of her that were lost. Eli saw the pain in his brother's face. They knew their grandmother from before, so strong and independent, was gone. The wiry old spitfire, quick with a quip, was now quiet and sad. There was a distant gaze in her eyes that told the boys she knew what was lost, but didn't know how to get it back.

Eli wanted to cry. What good would it do though? No tears could bring back what was gone. The hollow feeling could never be filled, not without some return to the way things were. But that just couldn't happen. So complete were the changes to the woman seated on the couch that memories of who she was may as well never have existed. The woman who returned from the hospital was not his grandma, that woman died a long time ago.

Eric seemed to have some vain hope of a return to normalcy, Eli thought. He was so adamant on doing what he could to remedy the past, that it seemed like he was oblivious to the real situation. But then, Eli would see the look in his eyes, that dead stare of reality setting in. Then he knew, Eric had lost all hope too. He operated mechanically. Even though at times it seemed there was a spark of hope, Eli knew, it was nothing more than a sputtering flame in the embers of a dying fire.

Eli wondered if it would have been better to just send grandma back to the nursing home. This was untenable. This lifestyle would quickly run its course and she would end up in an assisted care facility sooner rather than later. Though she was already dead, she clung too firmly to life to actually let go. What was she holding to? What was left to live for? This wasn't who she wanted to be, Eli was certain of that, but she couldn't let go. Was it really even her? Was she there still clutching to the last months of life or had her body betrayed her, killed the mind and usurped the body? For years her mind had staved off the ills of time, but in absence of that controlling power, the body withered away to nothing. A slow death was a tragic thing.

Better to be gone in a flash, burned out in the twinkling of an eye. That's where tears came from, Eli thought. When you burn so bright and are gone before anyone can even say goodbye. The tears come seeking that once familiar light only to find that it is gone. Tears are memories of a burning star, streaking across the sky before disappearing in a blaze, all too soon.

But not this, this lingering, lost existence. Why hold on to this? Eli stared at the woman seated on the couch. Eric leaned against the wall. He stared blankly into space. It was an expression Eli remembered keenly from when his brother was drunk. That sort of lost and lonely ambivalence, an uncaring, disinterested sort of gaze.

Eli thought he could understand. What was there here? What was this? This miserable half-life, alive but not living. Alive in one sense, but dead in all that mattered. What was this? There had to be something more. How could someone continue like this for any length of time?

No, he was going down that rabbit hole again. He couldn't venture too far down that path. It was too easy to get lost and spiral out of control. Leave it, go someplace else, he thought. Think happy thoughts. Think happy thoughts.

But there was nothing to be happy about. Cali was gone. The one single spark that could light his day was missing. He couldn't do this, all of this, empty living, on and on, day after day. For what? What was at the end of this tunnel?

He needed to leave.

He stood, leaning heavily on his crutch. Eric watched. Eli met his eyes briefly, long enough to say he couldn't stay. Eric understood, he nodded, his lips pinched in a thin line. Eli hobbled out the front door and onto the steps. He was breathless by the time he sat down. He was weak and getting weaker. He really did need to move more. But not right now. Now, he needed to sit.

Just like the neighbors down the street, here he sat with nothing to do, nothing to work towards or be. This was it, whatever this moment was, sitting on a porch watching a dead-end street.

A wave of heat passed through him. Eli was suddenly light headed. The street before him became blindingly bright. He closed his eyes and buried his face in his hands. He breathed slowly, counting to five and exhaling.

What's wrong? He thought.

He opened his eyes and stared at the step below. Faded blue paint weathered from years of sun and snow, greeted him. The wooden step was chipped and warped. The middle segment was completely bare.

How many times had he run down these stairs? He had jumped down onto the cement below, skipping the last step completely and tearing off on some adventure. Lord knows how many times he trod this step as he made off for Cali's. Now, he could barely take the steps without falling. He wanted to run, back to the days when life made sense. He couldn't stay here. He was living in a place he just didn't belong.

He closed his eyes again. He tried to imagine something, anything but here. Where would he go? Where could he go? If he was healed and there were no limits, where would he go? Where would Cali have wanted to go? A lake, no a beach, somewhere warm. The sun would glisten on her skin. Her shy freckles that only appeared at the coaxing of the summer sun would dot her cheeks and nose. Her green eyes were lively and warm as she watched the waves.

"Come dance with me?" she asked, both a question and a statement. "Come dance, no one can stop us here, nothing can stop us."

Complete freedom. An expanding horizon stretched out into nothing, everything. The golden sun bleeding out on the sea, the red hues mingled with blue, the massive expanse of ocean made everything else seem small. That freedom, unattached to anything he currently knew. The great wide open. A life without limits.

That's where Cali belonged. She was too perfect for this place.

"Eli, let's go," she whispered, soft and smooth.

There was nothing he would rather do, than leave with her.

Leave all this behind and melt into a summer sunset with Cali.

He imagined her smile, the sunlight giving a warm glow to her soft features. She was beautiful. He had always thought that, but imagining her as she was, as she always had been and would be, he was struck by just how attractive she really was. A far cry from the bitter ugliness of this town. There was a vibrant life-giving force in his imaginings that this reality couldn't contain. In his thoughts Cali existed as she truly was, vibrant, energetic, and alive. That was the truth. Not this washed out morose existence. This was something else. A lie? A simulation? A dream? No, none of those made sense. Disappointing and irritating, yes, but how could this life be a lie? He could reach out and touch the things around him. He could feel pain physically and emotionally. He felt the sun on his face this very moment. No, this wasn't a lie, but there was something. An inconsistency, something lacking, a hollow void that screamed for Eli's attention. It was more than just Cali's absence, there was something more. Something else. When set up against his imagination, when compared, only one felt real. Only one existed as things were supposed to be. There was more though, something was wrong.

If Cali was true. And in spite of all he was told, if she was alive, then what was this? What was he living, if the truth only existed in his mind? What was he doing in this place? This gray doldrum. He shook his head, he was going out of his mind.

Eli glanced at his wrist, a black leather banded watch was loosely latched. He unbuckled the latch and tightened the band. Turning his hand over he glanced at the time. The watch face was blank. There were no hour or minute markers. The hands were overlapped pointing toward what would be 8 o'clock if there had been a marker. But something else caught his eye at that moment. The second hand. It wasn't ticking properly. It ticked slowly, one, two, three, and pause. One, two, pause. One, pause. Slowly, it came to a halt. Eli waited, but the ticking hand had come to a complete stop.

He turned his attention away for a moment and caught something strange in the corner of his eye. As his eyes left his watch, the hand gently inched backward. Eli returned his full attention to the timepiece. But the hand refused to move.

Again, he looked away. Then barely noticeable, he saw it. The hand ticked backward. One, two, three. Tick, tick, tick. The hand inched back in time. The seconds shed from history like leaves from a tree, or maybe, like dead leaves brought back to life, growing back returning to full bloom. Turning backward, farther and faster, to a moment that should never have happened. A moment, Eli thought, that might not have happened.

Suddenly, a tremor started in his neck and raced down his spine. His body shook. His eyes burned, the dull gray street turned a glaring white. He struggled to his feet, he was weak beyond reason. The air caught in his lungs. He steadied himself and slowly exhaled. His breath escaped in bursts and sputters.

What happened?

He stumbled inside, everything was spinning. He couldn't make sense of the room, it was all shadows. He leaned on his crutch. A deep breath did little good. He shivered uncontrollably. He wanted to call out to Eric, but just speaking seemed an impossible task with the way his body trembled.

Eli slumped onto the couch. A weight seemed to bear down upon him. His head was heavy, his body listless.

Everything was dark and sound seemed far off. Was he having a seizure? Dying?

What the hell happened?

He had been doing nothing. Sitting. Thinking. And that was all he could do now, sit and think. Maybe he could organize his thoughts. Maybe there was something that could explain this sudden onslaught. What else could he call it. It was an attack, or maybe it was all in his mind, either way, nothing seemed right. Or maybe, maybe it was just him, maybe he was off. But why? He racked his brain trying to make some sense of a senseless moment. But there was nothing that could explain it. He had done nothing.

He continued to think. There had to be something. He tried to recall his thoughts, thoughts of Cali and his dreams and life. Life without her. Without her beauty, without her truth. He stopped. The word seemed to stand out in his mind. Truth. That, that was it. The truth.

He touched a nerve, some heartstring to the fabric of reality. He plucked just a little too keenly, vibrating the chord of life to its very core. The very essence of his being screamed out in terror. The truth hidden behind a shroud of seeming reality fought to regain control of the illusion, but like a magician flailing to reign in an audience after a failed trick, there was no turning back. Eli was awake to the world around him. He knew what was behind the curtain.

He had stumbled upon an answer that he didn't understand. He saw something he wasn't supposed to and the universe was trying to push him away from it, away from whatever truth he had found. A question blazed in Eli's mind, if he had discovered a hidden truth, a different reality, what was he to do with it? Was there anything he could do? Was there a way to bridge the gap between this life and that? There had to be, there had to be a way back there.

"Eli wake up," her voice, soft and sweet whispered in his ear. Truth.

"Cali."

He could see her, through the darkness, through the fog of illusion, he could picture her. The room around her glowed red and orange, her tear stained face pleading for him to come back, to wake up, to return to life. She was waiting for him. It's what he wanted, what he felt was true. It had to be true.

He just had to reach out and take her hand, then, open his eyes. She would be there, alive as she was supposed to be. How long had it been?

Hours. Days. Years. Time was nothing in light of the truth, just please, please, please, don't go. Don't leave me to wander in the dark, a lie feigning reality. Not that. Please, not that, Eli thought. I can't live knowing the truth is somewhere out there beyond my grasp, mocking me, showing but a glimpse of itself like a memory that never happened, true in a sense, but false in every other way. Tell me that isn't this. Please. Tell me you're really there.

"Eli."

She spoke soft, fading in the distance.

No. No. No! He screamed in his head. Don't take her away! Don't leave!

"Eli."

Her voice was nothing more than a whisper.

"Cali, Cali wait," he tried to call, his voice failed him. He wanted to tell her, he saw her. He heard her. But she was already gone.

Chapter 33

Eli blinked. Images from a daydream mingled with the world around him before disappearing. He was close that time, he felt it. He was getting better at directing his mind, but he still lacked complete control. With each passing day, he felt closer to the truth, closer to holding on to the dream and directing it. Once he could do that, he could discover the truth, he could find out what was real.

The dreary street stretched on ahead, turning fuzzy in the distance. The heat rippled waves of radiation and the stagnant smell of cigarettes hung on the air. Such was life. This was the home Eli had always known.

He sighed. There was nothing more to see here he thought as he slowly stood. Nothing, as always. How did they do it? Just keep on keeping on, he thought. Was that the end he was destined for? Some old dude sitting on his front porch watching the world drift by? He shuddered, what pains had caused such apathy that life was just the few feet of lawn and the quarter mile segment of desolate pavement?

There was something better out there.

He turned his back to the street and wandered back inside. It took a minute for his eyes to adjust. Eric was somewhere, in the kitchen, Eli heard plates and cups clanking in the sink. His grandmother was still motionless on the couch. Her face came into focus as Eli's eyes acclimated to the dimly lit room. She looked pale. Even her eyes had taken on a lifeless gray hue. Eli shook his head as he remembered what she used to be like. Those eyes had never seemed so dead. She was old, always had been in Eli's eyes, but she never seemed old until now. There were no sharp replies, no keen wisdom. This was it.

Eli felt a pang of guilt as a thought crossed his mind. The corner of his mouth pinched in a frown.

He shuffled out to the kitchen and took a seat at the table. Eric didn't stop doing dishes, Eli saw his head turn, but he didn't say anything.

"What now?" Eli asked.

Eric continued washing dishes.

Eli turned his eyes to the table. He gazed at the wood, dark lines formed odd shaped rings in the grain. What part of the tree had this been? Probably the trunk. Maybe a branch, Eli thought.

"What do you mean?" Eric said after a time.

"I don't know, just, what's the plan? What are we going to do?" Eli asked.

"We?" Eric turned from the dishes to face Eli. "I'll work. We'll have to hire home help or something for grandma. And you, you are going to continue going to therapy and get your leg healed. You're gonna be walking again soon, without the crutch."

Eli glanced up. The light through the window cast a blue light around his brother.

"Where will you work?" he asked.

"I don't know. Probably the factory. It pays alright," Eric said.

"Yea, that's good."

"You want to talk about grandma though," Eric said.

"Yea. It's just, I don't know. You see it right? She's not the same," Eli said.

"No, she isn't," Eric agreed. He dried his hands and sat down in the chair across from Eli. "She will never be the same. It's my fault. If I had done something sooner, they might have been able to do something. This is on me. So, I gotta do what I can to make it right, even though it's never gonna be right."

Eli bit his lip.

"What?" Eric said.

"It's just, do you think she's happy here?"

"You mean, would she be better at the nursing home?" Eric asked.

Eli shrugged.

"No, screw that. This is her home. It's been her home for sixty some years. She doesn't want to leave," Eric said. "She's like this because I messed up. I'm not going to send her away. She stays here. If that means I need to work two jobs to pay for a home care nurse, so be it. I'm not sending here away because its hard on me."

"But don't you think she'd be happier?" Eli asked.

"Eli, stop. She'd be happy if she was like she used to be. But she's not. And she won't be happy, here or in a nursing home," Eric said. "So, I'm not going to send her someplace to die. She can stay here, where she's comfortable. This is her home. I'm not gonna send her off to die somewhere else."

Eric's eyes were filled with tears, his cheeks were red. The blue light around him seemed denser somehow. Eli felt the pain in his words. But there was nothing more to say. This is how it was going to be.

He nodded.

"I'm sorry," he said.

"Me too."

The evening passed slowly. Eli and Eric didn't talk again. What was the point? Eli grew uncomfortable downstairs and hobbled up to his room and waited for sleep to take him.

The hours dragged by. When he finally felt tired enough to sleep, he closed his eyes gladly and slipped into that other place. A place where everything felt right.

Part of him wanted to drift away to nothingness, to let go, forget everything, let the dream have its way with him. But another part of him wanted control over what came next. This was the true test, could he maintain control? Whether it was a dream or a glimpse of another life, if he could just hold on to it, control it, maybe he could find some peace. He deserved some semblance of peace, right? Even just for a minute, could he just have this one thing? Something worthwhile to hold on to.

She stepped forward, a ghost. Her bright green eyes, watched him cautiously. Now was his time, this was his chance.

"Cali," he said. The words slipped off his tongue easily. He took a hesitant step forward. Then another and another. Cali remained standing, waiting to see if he was willing to make his dreams reality. With each conscious step, Eli became aware of the control he had. It was a feeling of complete liberty. Gone were the days of chasing shadows. He ventured into a world of his choosing and there was no turning back.

He took Cali's hands in his. She smiled.

"I was worried, you would never come back," she said.

"I'm here now," Eli answered wrapping his arms around her.

"I'm glad you're here."

"Me too."

Cali looked him in the eye.

"Promise you won't leave again," she said.

"I don't want to."

A soft smile passed from Cali's face.

"I thought you were dead," she said.

The words sent a shiver down his spine. She had said that before or something like it. He didn't understand. He didn't want to. He just wanted to make this moment last forever, let everything else fade away. But something about her words stuck with him. What if?

What if this wasn't a dream at all? This moment, every moment with her, what if that existed somewhere else, somewhere away from his dreams? Someplace real?

What if Cali was alive?

And he was dead.

"Do I seem dead to you?" he asked.

"No, but. . ."

"No," he said. "I'm right here."

"I want this to be real, more than anything," Cali said.

"Then don't fight what's right in front of you," Eli replied. He felt his grip over this moment slipping. "I'm right here. Alive. Let that be enough. Whatever happened, is in the past. This is right now."

She smiled.

"Then let's go," she said.

They took off down the road, over the hilltop and on down to the river. They kicked off their shoes at the water's edge and waded into the stream. The water was cool and refreshing. Minnows scurried out from beneath the slippery stones as Eli and Cali waded deeper. Small fish investigated the disturbance, but quickly jettisoned away.

There wasn't a cloud in the sky. Cicadas sang from the trees as the sun baked the earth below. The heat was a welcome friend, burning away any negativity. Eli felt command of the moment return to him.

This was life. Everything felt right. When their lips touched, that was true. Eli felt it. More than anything he could remember, this was life. He wouldn't let go.

The sun shined endlessly, the world drifted to nothing on the periphery. Nothing mattered besides this moment. *Don't go.* Nothing else ever mattered when he was with Cali. It was always that way, always had been. She was summer. *Don't go.*

Everything slowed down, each movement. Every feeling exaggerated. There was no time, they could take forever.

Lightning flashed. It ripped through the summer sky, one brilliant static charge fast and full of fury. The bullwhip snap of nature's power struck quick to the core. The rolling echo of thunder followed close behind.

Storm clouds blocked the sun, converging quickly overhead, threatening to explode at any moment.

No, not a storm, not now, Eli thought. He wasn't going to lose this perfect moment.

"Rain, rain, go away," he whispered.

Cali watched him. A smile tugged at the corner of her lips.

"Rain, rain, go away," she repeated.

"Come again another day," Eli sang, laughter bubbled up as the words left his lips. They continued on together.

"Rain, rain, go away, come again another day."

A streak of light cut through the heavy storm clouds. The glimmering sun cast rainbows of color in every direction. Raindrops that had only begun their decent burst in vibrant flashes of color. The water droplets were like tiny fireworks popping above their heads.

The clouds rolled away. Blue sky returned. The last rain particles floated off in the distance, their vibrant colors reflected in the teens' eyes. The sun was high overhead once more, the heat returned.

"Did we?" Eli left off.

"I think so," Cali said.

Eli laughed.

"We can do anything we want," Cali said.

"I like that."

"No, it's true," she said. She ventured out deeper into the stream. Eli followed, the water rose up to their hips. Cold but welcome beneath the summer sun.

"Anything we want, Eli," Cali said. "Close your eyes."

Eli smiled, but did as she said.

She stepped closer her hand brushed against his thigh.

"It's hot, the sun is shining. It's unmistakably summer, right?" she said.

"Mhm," Eli agreed.

"Then how is this possible?" Cali said as something cold touched Eli's cheek.

He opened his eyes. There before him, dazzling white snowflakes fluttered all around. Soft flakes, floated overhead melting as they touched Eli's skin. He looked at Cali, her hair shined beneath a glossy layer of snow.

She smiled.

Then taking his hands she pulled him close. Eli leaned forward anticipating a kiss, but suddenly he was underwater. The shock scared his eyes open, Cali swam to his left. Eli stood, streams of cool water trickled down his face as he emerged from the river. A little distance away Cali raised her head. The water was deeper where she was. She bobbed slightly up and down as she floated there. She beckoned Eli to join her. He laughed and followed her. He couldn't touch bottom, so, he kicked to stay afloat. Cali smiled as he drew near. Her hair stuck to the sides of her face and neck. Her green eyes shined bright against the blue water.

A snowflake fell between them and dissolved as it touched the water.

Eli shook his head and smiled.

"Anything is possible. Anything we want," Cali said.

This is what he longed for. This escape, the freedom of this moment. Alone, away from all the world. No trouble, no problems. A perfect oasis, what summer was supposed to be.

But it was too perfect. He knew that. This life was impossible. But if they never acknowledged it. If they never spoke about it, maybe they could live the lie.

Cali's eyes met his. She inched closer. As if reading his thoughts, she spoke.

"Eli, this isn't real."

The blood stopped cold in his veins. Don't say that, he wanted to argue.

"This isn't real. I know that, but I still want this. I want you here," she said.

"No," Eli said.

"It's okay. This is what you want right?" she asked.

"Cali, just stop."

"What?"

"Just don't say it again."

"That none of this is real?"

The word struck hard. Reality, it was what he was searching for and yet Cali threw the word around like nothing. He knew this wasn't real. But he could have pretended, he could have swept the truth aside, if it meant he could live like this a little longer.

"Well it's not," she said. "I know that. I mean, you've been dead for months."

Eli's heart stopped.

"What?"

Cali watched him closely, her green eyes searching him for something.

"What did you say?" he asked.

"Eli, we both know the truth. But it's okay. We are here now."

"No, no, Cali. I'm right here. I'm still here," Eli said.

Cali was silent.

He took her hand.

"Do I feel dead?"

Tears welled in her eyes.

"Eli," she whispered. "I just miss you so much. I want this to be real. Why can't this be our life? Why do I only get to see you in my dreams?"

She stole the words from out of his mouth. Why couldn't their dreams be their reality?

Cali leaned her head on Eli's chest.

"I wish you were here for real," she said.

"I know."

"Can we keep this? Even if it isn't real, I don't want to let go," she said.

"This can be our escape," Eli said.

"Forever?"

"And always."

Chapter 34

"Eli, I would like to talk about something we haven't really touched on yet," Dr. Guevait said. "If you are comfortable with that."

Eli picked at his fingernail. His eyes were focused on a thin strip of skin next to his nail. The skin was hardened and frayed, ready to be cast away. Eli struggled to grip the flesh with his fingers. He wanted to bite it, a quick nibble and it would be gone. But he wouldn't do that. No, the nagging flesh remained as he lifted his eyes to Dr. Guevait.

"Ok," he said.

"Tell me about Cali," Dr. Guevait said.

Eli's eyes narrowed.

"Why?"

"We have talked about a lot of things. We've talked about the wreck, your grandma, your brother, but we haven't talked about Cali," Dr. Guevait said. "I get the impression she is integral to this story. But, you have been reluctant to talk of her."

Eli turned his attention back to his nail.

"There's not much to say," he mumbled.

"Why's that?"

Eli bit his lip and glanced at the door.

"She's not here," he said quietly.

"She's not here, now," Dr. Guevait said. "But she was. And you were close to her."

Eli nodded.

"Yea. How do you feel when you think of her?"

Eli thought of his dreams. Of what he really thought when he was with her. Everything, almost everything, felt perfect. It felt right when he was with her. But here, none of that made sense. Those feelings were distant.

"I don't think of her often," he said.

"Really? Well, when you do, what are your thoughts?"

Eli focused his eyes on Dr. Guevait. The man was soft around the middle, his hair was curly, but thinning at the top of his head. His eyes were kind and sympathetic. He was listening, waiting.

Eli breathed deep.

"I miss her," he said simply before looking away. "Nothing feels right without her here."

"Mhm," the doctor nodded.

"It's hard to explain, everything just feels off."

"Right, no, that makes sense," Dr. Guevait said.

Eli caught the doctor's eyes. He really was listening.

"It's more than that, though," Eli said.

"Ok."

"Sometimes, I have dreams. Cali is there, you know?" he started. "And it feels right, like that's the way things are supposed to be."

The doctor nodded.

"That's understandable," he said.

"But it makes me wonder," Eli said. Then he hesitated.

Dr. Guevait waited.

"It makes me wonder, if really that is the way things are supposed to be. What if all this is wrong?"

"All this?" Dr. Guevait asked.

Eli waved his hands in front of him. "All this. Like, is this it? My girlfriend is dead so here I am, going to therapy, waiting to die."

"Whoa, Eli, let's slow down for a second okay?" Dr. Guevait said.

Eli laughed.

"In case ya didn't notice, my leg's still broken. I'm not going anywhere fast."

"No, I'm just. When you say things like that. . ." Dr. Guevait trailed off.

"What? Wanting to die?" Eli responded. "Am I wrong? In one way or another that's what we're all doing."

"In a philosophical way, yes. I know what you mean. But I have to ask, you haven't had thoughts of suicide, have you?" Dr. Guevait asked.

Eli was silent. Cali's voice whispered in his ear, *"You've been dead for weeks."* Maybe his subconscious was speaking through her in his dreams. Maybe his subconscious mind was guiding his dreams, leading him towards some acceptance of Cali's death. Or maybe somewhere far off in a parallel universe he really was dead and Cali was alive. He imagined a cold bright room, a hospital bed and a lone chair. Thick cotton sheets were laid over a body. A young woman was seated in the chair. She held his hand. Then a harsh bell rang. Cali jumped. She screamed, but her words were drowned out. The scene dissolved.

Dr. Guevait watched him, waiting.

I'm already dead. I've been dead since the day Cali died, Eli thought. The only thing I'm living for is dreams of her. Tell me, is that living, doc? It feels a lot like dying. Slow and agonizing, day by day just withering away, drifting further from reality, toward another truth. Another life. I'm already dead, that's what he wanted to say.

Instead, he shook his head and smiled.

"No," he said. "I'm not suicidal. I don't want to die, but everyone does."

Dr. Guevait wrote something on his notepad. When he finished writing he looked up and met Eli's gaze.

"Good. That's good," he said. "Obviously, we don't want that for you. But those thoughts would be understandable after your experience. If you were having those thoughts, I just want you to know it's okay to talk to me about it. That's what I'm here for, to help you grapple with those difficult thoughts. There's no shame here, Eli. We can talk about anything."

Eli turned his attention to the floor and mumbled thanks.

"We were talking about Cali and your thoughts. Do you want to continue that conversation?"

Eli lifted his head, "What do you want to know?"

"The floor is yours, Eli. I want nothing. If you want to talk, that's fine. If not, that's fine too."

"I guess. I don't know. It's just hard."

Eli paused.

"I guess, it's just hard to accept she's not here," Eli said.

Dr. Guevait nodded.

"I didn't expect she would be gone like this, you know?" Eli said. "She was smart, beautiful, funny. She had a future. And now, that's all gone."

Dr. Guevait wrote in his notebook. The he looked up.

"Maybe," he said. "Maybe she is gone, but it doesn't mean she hasn't impacted your life. Changed you somehow. Changed who you are."

"What do you mean?"

"Tell me who you are, Eli," Dr. Guevait said.

Eli gazed at the doctor. He picked at his nail, the stubborn skin clung tight.

Finally, after too long sitting in silence he muttered, "I don't know."

"Are you saying that to avoid answering or because you really don't know the answer?"

"I don't know," Eli replied.

"That's alright. I think that's where we should stop today. You should take some time and think about it. You might not have an answer right now, or even a year from now. My hope is that eventually you'll find the answer to that question. And that will lead you somewhere."

Eli nodded. Then, he turned his face away from Dr. Guevait and quickly bit his hangnail, the skin broke free easily.

Chapter 35

Who am I?

The question shook Eli. In all this time, he had beat around that one important question. He was always looking for an escape, a way out, chasing a dream that could never be reached. But through it all he hadn't stopped to think who he was, or better, who he wanted to be. Now, he couldn't stop thinking about it.

Who am I?

Eli kicked that question around all evening without coming to any definitive answer.

His notebook was splayed open before him. He flipped through the pages. Dreams upon dreams. Each one came back in vivid detail as he read over the entries. Like memories plucked from another life, Eli remembered everything. Every dream felt real enough to touch, there was no separation from "reality". Whether it happened in a dream or not, it was all real.

Yet, Eli knew that the allure of sleep was the freedom it provided. He wanted to cling to that freedom. He wanted to trade his waking hours for an eternity of that freedom.

Dr. Gueviat's question rang in his ear. Who am I?

Would this be his life? Would he spend every waking moment itching for that escape, knowing that it would never last? Was that living? Longing for something that could never be?

He thought of Eric and suddenly Eli could understand how his brother used to drink. Searching for an escape looked crazy from the outside, but in the middle of that journey paradise seemed within arm's reach.

The tip of his pen rested on the page.

Who am I?

There wasn't an answer, so Eli wrote the question over again. And again. Each time, he considered it and really thought over it, but to what end? There wasn't an answer. Or maybe he just didn't want to write the truth.

The thought was like a light in a dark room. His dreams with Cali were his escape, it was his way of avoiding the truth of who he really was. If he could just distract himself with a perfect world where Cali was alive and everything felt right, then he wouldn't have to face the reality of who he was.

He read over his last dream entry. He could hear Cali's voice and he knew the dreams of her would never go away. But they couldn't be his reason for living. No, he needed to find purpose elsewhere.

He needed to write the truth. He needed to confront who he really was, then maybe he could find something worth living for.

Who am I? he wrote. Then he let the truth guide his pen.

I am. . .

Lonely.

Weak.

Depressed.

Lazy.

Bored.

Empty.

A list of adjectives. Accurate, but not an answer to the question. Who am I? He listed characteristics, but that wasn't enough. No one was anything all the time.

I'm not always lonely or depressed, Eli thought. Those are pieces of me, but not the whole. There had to be more, something to work toward, something to do, to be. But what?

Again, who am I? What do I want? Who do I want to be?

Nothing. No one.

He slapped his notebook shut. This wasn't going anywhere.

A new thought came to him from the hazy recesses of his mind. Don't focus on facts alone, just write, spill it out on the page, let it be what it's going to be, the truth would be there.

So, he did. He wrote. First, the weather, then the heat, what summer felt like and how it made him think of her and what she was like and what it was like when they were together and how it was hard to cope with her absence and that question that seemed to plague him. Was she really dead? How could she be? He saw her all the time, but he saw plenty of things that weren't real, but there was something that felt real, true, but what was truth? What was real and what was memory?

He closed his eyes. Colors darted before him, reds, blues, purples, and oranges. He couldn't put everything together, but it felt like there was something, a feeling or emotion tied to each color.

He opened his eyes. He was about to write, but there were no words. The tip of his pen rested on the page. It was a feeling; no words would do it justice. His memories of Cali, of her life, of their time, they were no more or less true than anything else he experienced.

Truth did not exist in concrete certainty. It was fluid, ephemeral, memories and feelings intertwined to form some view of the world. A life-shaping, identity-defining reality that was different for everyone, but somehow tied together loosely. His own memories were tied to Cali, just as hers had been tied to him. And even if she was gone, who was to say her memory didn't live on? In fact, Eli would make sure it did. Cali was more than a dream or a memory, she was life. Through his memories of her, Eli fought for something more. He couldn't let her become numbers on a tombstone. She was more than that. For so long she had been his reason for living, and without her he didn't know what he wanted. But remaining lonely and trying to escape from reality wasn't the life she would have wanted for him. He was wrong, he was searching for something he would never find and she was trying to show him that. He wanted a life with her, but he couldn't have that. She was gone. But a life for her? That was different, a life for her memory.

He wouldn't let her die. He would make sure she lived on, in his heart, in his memories, and in the hearts and memories of everyone that read her story.

Her story needed to be told and he was the one to say it.

He couldn't wallow in this misery, he had to use it, make something beautiful from tragedy. Cali deserved that. She deserved so much more. But if he could show the importance of every single moment, of cherishing life while it's here. If he could just communicate the importance of loving while life remained, then there was something to live for.

But it couldn't be just that. That was a start. But Cali wouldn't have wanted Eli to live just for her, would she? Not her alone anyways.

She would have wanted him to find something, some passion that drove him to be better. To leave this town. To make something. To do something.

That was out there. Whatever it was. It was out there.

Maybe it started with a story. Her story. Their love. Not something made up, but the real story. Their love was an endless summer. No dreams. That's what he wanted to write, to start with anyway. Write it like it was, like it happened.

From there, anything could happen. Maybe there were other stories yet to be discovered. Maybe there were deeper truths about himself that would come to life. There was a world of possibilities he could explore. There was a life to live and stories to be told. It started with this one, the one where he wakes up and starts living the dream.